Good Grief!

Terrie Sizemore

Printed in the United States of America
A 2 Z Press LLC
PO Box 582
Deleon Springs, FL 32130
bestlittleonlinebookstore.com
sizemore3630@aol.com
440-241-3126
ISBN: 978-1-954191-77-8

DEDICATION:

*To all those who have
experienced grief and
to those who will
at sometime*

Contents

Foreword

Grief – Grief is no stranger to most of us who have lost someone we truly love. Good Grief! Is a short story about a woman who lost someone very close to her and had difficulty letting go. She copes in a unique manner as her family and friends see the difficulty she is experiencing and they patiently and kindly bring her to the reality of her loss, help her with her grief experience, and watch her continue to enjoy life despite the sorrow she's faced and learned to treasure each and every moment with the ones she loves and treasure each moment she herself has in this world. Ride along and laugh and cry with her as she takes her journey here.

This little story is about grief, just like the title tells us. In fact, it's about *Good Grief.* How can that be? Grief is a normal process each one of us experiences when we experience loss.

At some time or another, each of us will experience grief.

1

How it all Began

'When's your next day off?' Tommy asked.

'Next Thursday,' I replied.

Tommy always had something special planned for the few days I had off work. To be honest, I was working too many hours a week. Veterinary work was booming in Florida and I couldn't pass up the opportunity to work since I was unable to find work in Ohio.

Looking back, I was amazed it had been six years since I came to Florida. Originally, I came because I thought I was only going to be here for five or six months. About four years before I decided to come to Florida, my best friend, Tommy, was given a terminal diagnosis. He came back to Ohio to say 'goodbye' to me and all his friends. He made amends where he thought he needed to and shared how the doctors told him he was never going to get better and would eventually die. He served in the military and was now a disabled veteran with a heart condition and failing lungs. I watched him walk slowly from my front door to his van and drive away. Sometimes I wish there were more words between us. Real words. Meaningful words. But I guess he didn't know what to say exactly and I didn't either. The only thing he said was, 'I had a good life.'

To which I replied, 'But, it's only half a life.' He was only fifty years old. I always assumed each and every one of us would have one hundred years of life. I am wrong. I realize no one gets to pick how long they live. Well, most don't, I guess.

For those four years before I came to Florida, I made a special effort to come several times a year to spend time with Tommy. We were best friends as children and continued our friendship into adulthood. My parents treated him like he was just one of the family. He moved to Florida many years before I came.

Tommy made so much of my visits. He picked me up at the airport and we had dinner and he told me of his list of things he planned while I was in Florida. It was always quite a long list. I enjoyed every moment.

Another time, Dad picked me up and Mom and Tommy were with him. We went straight from the airport to Blue Springs in Orange City, Florida. Our wetsuits and snorkeling gear were packed. When we arrived at the spring, we dressed and Tommy and I hopped into the water and began snorkeling from one point on the river to the area called the *headspring*. This is where the water comes out in large volumes every minute of every day and feeds the spring run and flows into the St. Johns River. Snorkeling was just one of the Florida activities Tommy introduced me to.

As we snorkeled, I was surprised by a large grey object swimming past me on my right. It was a manatee!! I had visited Florida so many times to catch sight of the manatees and was never able to due to the time of year. Manatees only come into the springs in cooler weather when the ocean water temperatures drop. The temperature in the springs is always seventy-two degrees, so they are warmer there.

I immediately began to make squeaking and undecipherable noises in my snorkel trying to get Tommy's attention. My mother said she heard me on the land as she walked the path close to the spring where we were snorkeling. She knew my strange noises meant I had seen a manatee.

Manatees are excellent swimmers and even though it looked at me as it swam, it quickly passed me and made its way to the headspring. I was excited but wanted more time with this beautiful creature. As Tommy and I continued snorkeling, the manatee returned to where we were and swam around and around us. I watched it swim close to us with the most delight I have ever experienced.

She, or he, wouldn't allow me to touch her or him, but she or he, was close. We are not permitted to touch them anyway because there are strict laws protecting manatees, but it was a special treat to finally see one; and so up close and personal. And, where was my underwater camera when I needed it?

When we finished our time in the water, we walked down a wooden boardwalk that allowed us to walk near the spring run to the St. Johns River. When we arrived where the spring joins the river, we spotted a ten-to-twelve-foot gator swimming in the direction of where we were just in the water. I vowed to never snorkel again, but I have; always on the lookout for dangling gator legs.

One particular visit, however, is indelibly inscribed in my memory. My sister and mother took me to the airport to catch my flight to Ohio. As we sat talking, Tommy called. He said how much he enjoyed my visit. His voice sounded sad and my friend tried to never be sad. I told him how much I enjoyed the visit as well.

When I finished the call, my mother said, 'He really misses you when you leave. He loves the time you spend with him. He's lonely.'

It was at that moment I knew I had to come. My friend needed me but didn't know how to ask. So, I left the only home I ever knew and traveled one thousand miles away from home and my friends and everything I loved to come to a place I never thought I would live.

I was born and lived in Ohio all my life before the move. I had so much fun training and racing harness horses, riding dressage and jumping horses, craft shopping with my favorite aunt, having holiday dinners with friends, and living on my thirty-acre farm. My best friends those days were the Amish neighbors that did everything for me.

Tommy was always a faithful friend when I was growing up and my parents took a liking to him as well. Once I thought I was sweet on him, but then realized he was a great friend and I didn't want to lose that. I had several failed romances and thought there was truly nothing keeping me in Ohio, so, I asked God to help me make the move.

Despite how much fun I had living in Ohio, after I turned fifty, they just didn't want me at work anymore. Times were difficult, to say the least. I was on the verge of losing everything I owned, including my farm. I had incurred huge credit card debt, still owed on my farm and truck, and needed a job. I resorted to selling all my horses and placing many of my eleven dogs in new homes that could love and care for them better than I was able to at the time. I didn't leave for these reasons though. Funny how we sometimes hold on when we should be letting go.

Before I moved, I thought I had a full life in Ohio and never intended to move, but apparently, God had other plans. One of my very favorite things, while I was still in Ohio, was to hang with my brother-in-law, Rick. He and my sister lived in Florida. He was always alone on Friday and Saturday nights when she went to work. So, every

Friday and Saturday, I did all my chores and running around and, after all was done, we hung out together on the phone. What did we ever do before cell phones?

Some days we'd look up at the stars in the sky – which came out about twenty minutes earlier for him - and I could never convince him that this was so. He figured they should come out at the same time. I'm no astronomer, but I realized he was about twenty minutes East of me, so my time was the same on the clock, but not for the sun.

After we discussed this at length every weekend, we'd turn our concentration to the stars. He was very bright and knew the names of constellations and more. I just pretended to know something about the stars and made noises to affirm how brilliant he was. We talked of how it would be when I finally moved to Florida and could look at the stars together. It seemed like a dream at the time. Like I said before, Ohio was the only home I had ever known.

Some nights Rick and I would pick a movie to watch together, one thousand miles away. How we managed this was if I had the disc, he would order it on YouTube and we would get in sync and start the movie at the exact same time so we could talk about it as we watched. Sometimes I fell asleep and my poor brother-in-law was left to watch all by himself.

Everyone was excited for me to come to Florida and, after deciding to come, I worked for months becoming licensed as a nurse and veterinarian there. I knew I couldn't go many months without a paycheck.

When I finally arrived in Florida, since I hadn't been employed in a while and was new to the state, I still couldn't find work right away. My mom and dad took me to places to apply for work and, being turned away so many times in a day, was difficult to handle. After about thirteen stops one day, I asked Mom if we could quit looking for the day. I was exhausted. Finally, I was offered a job as a nurse in a nursing home and a large hospital on the coast. The ball was rolling and would soon be even more abundant.

The reason I thought I would only be in Florida for five or six months was because I came to spend the last months with my friend who was gravely ill. As I mentioned, Tommy had medical issues that resulted in him being labeled 'terminal.' But, since he was a trooper, he never gave up and we spent every day I had off doing something fun, even though there weren't many.

After being hired as a nurse and, since Tommy was doing amazingly well, I decided to stay in Florida a little longer. Things were going superbly. Rick and my sister were glad to have me close; especially Rick when Sher went to work. My parents were happy to have me. We were doing fun things like taking walks at the nearby refuge, seeing manatees, going to the beach, shopping in St. Augustine, and more. It meant so much to my friend to have me here. I could tell he needed me. He would never say, but I knew.

I put an ad for relief veterinary services and went to work! I could have worked 24/7 in Florida and no one cares how old I am! Very exciting for an old lady, I must admit. This resulted in months where I worked twenty-eight days and meant Tommy and I only had a few full days to make plans. After work, we watched Jeopardy in the evenings and Tommy joined the family for late suppers at Mom's, but he made special plans on my days off.

Another bonus to moving to Florida was that Rick and I no longer had to communicate by phone. We now made arrangements to do things when my sister went to work that included trips to the mall for shopping and treats. I rode on the frame of his motorized wheelchair as he sped through the parking lots to the mall. People were surprised by this but it was something normal to us. And to think I couldn't have any more fun than I was having in Ohio.

I am so thankful for the memories. Tommy also joined the fun and every weekend, we borrowed movies from the library and Tommy bought eats and we had a little party, just the three of us.

Tomorrow, however, Tommy and I were planning a trip to the river. It was my favorite five-mile run; Silver River in Silver Springs. Rick gifted us with a video camera and we took it wherever we went so we could share the experience with him. I forgot to mention that Rick is a paralyzed man and he lives in a wheelchair. He seems just like us in every other way, so I forget that part sometimes. We all make the best of every moment we have together.

To prepare for our adventure, I loaded both kayaks on the truck and tied them securely. Life jackets and whistles are required in Florida when on the rivers there. Tommy and I ate simply, so I had to decide on ham sandwiches with lots of mayonnaise for him or peanut butter and jelly.

As I combed the cupboards for our lunch items, I found everything I needed for peanut butter and jelly sandwiches. I made two for him and one for me. Tommy loved orange juice, so I added that to the cooler as well as the granola bars that were the standardly packed snacks he enjoyed.

Next, I made sure I included the sunscreen because, 'In Florida, we wear sunscreen every day that ends in 'Y!'' I softly said to myself and smiled as I remembered seeing those words at the Dermatologist's office a few months back with my father.

All packed. I set the alarm for 6 am. Tommy liked to leave early, so we would be the first ones on the river. Off to sleep, excited about the next day.

CANADA
OHIO
FLORIDA
MEXIC
N
MAP of the
UNITED STATES,
MARCH 15
(GOP EDITION)

2

The River

We set off early that morning. Tommy and I both agreed we'd have a better time if I drove. I am a terrible passenger. Ever since my near-fatal crash on icy roads in Ohio, I cannot bear to be a passenger in any vehicle unless the driver drives like some grandpa everyone else on the road, simply put, hates.

Since Tommy likes to talk with his hands, it makes me very nervous to have his hands off the wheel while we're driving. So, anyone can easily see why it's easier for me to just do the driving. Less stress. Less tension between us.

It's a forty-five-minute drive to the springs so I prepare myself for the same stories I have heard a million times. Stories of catching Gar fish and seeing gators surface next to his kayak. Stories of catching snapping turtles and leaving them go again and jumping out of moving vehicles to catch a snake crossing the road at Kelly's Island – and island in the waters of Lake Erie. Stories of him buying my mother a shirt with the words, 'Gator Bait' on the back. He and Mom spent many days on the rivers together before I came along.

I picked him up. 'Got everything?' I asked as he loaded his gear in the back of the truck.

'Yeah. I'll put my bag in the back. I brought the video camera so we can take pictures of everything. Maybe we'll see a huge gator today. Rick'll get a kick out of it. I'll narrate it like I'm on the hunt for the next biggest gator.'

We both laughed. Tommy is fearless. He knows I'm not. He puts up with me anyway. Once, he told me if I jumped off a ten-foot diving board into the Blue Springs on the Santa Fe River, he would buy me a very expensive bicycle. When I arrived at the springs and climbed the stairs to the diving board, I looked down into the crystal-clear water of the lovely springs and couldn't do it. I was chicken. Tommy coaxed me over and over and I still couldn't do it. He bought me the bicycle anyway. He was always doing things like that.

Well, today was a sunny, warm Florida day and I was going on the river with my best friend. When we arrived, I unloaded my kayak and put it close to the water. Tommy always took charge of his own. I went to pay as the lady asked, 'How many today?'

'Two, please,' I responded.

She looked at me and then behind me and to the right of my shoulder. She looked puzzled, but I told her Tommy would be along shortly. She nodded and gave me the armbands to prove payment.

As we set off, Tommy shared all his knowledge of the Springs and his escapades in Florida as he has done each and every time we enjoy the river together. I have knowledge I'm not sure will ever come in handy, but I enjoy the lively banter.

He showed me the high-water marks on the trees and told me that meant the water was that high at one time – usually with a hurricane storm. He talked about Kite birds and how he caught a young gator who was sunning itself on a log one trip. I loved the sound of his excited voice.

One more of the things I loved about being on the river with Tommy was that it always seemed like his 'first time.' He had the enthusiasm of a child and the courage of a giant. Each time we went it was never boring to him. His happiness always rubbed off. I wanted to look at life like that and have that same feeling even if I was doing the same thing for the one-thousandth time.

We glided with the strong current of the Silver River. We wouldn't even have to paddle but we'd crash into things if we didn't control which direction we floated along. In the first small run that takes kayakers and paddleboarders to the main river, we spotted a ten-foot gator sunning itself on the bank. I say, 'And to our left, is the first gator of the day. Sure hope he's not hungry yet this morning and he stays put there!'

Tommy smiles. He's not afraid of those gators the way I am. We continue to float down the short run and finally arrive at the main river. The water opens up into a large river that flows along continuously. As we make the turn, we join some other kayakers. 'Lovely day to be on the river,' one said to Tommy.

'Sure beats the hustle and bustle of the city,' Tommy responded.

We did love being outdoors where the sun shined over our backs and the sounds of nature were all around us. Blue herons walked on lily pads at the edge of the river. Cormorants dove for fish and then stepped out onto limbs of trees above the water to spread their wings to dry.

'Did you bring bananas in case we see monkeys?' I asked.

'I never leave home without them,' he replied.

As we floated a couple of miles down the river, we saw a group of turtles on a log. They ranged in size from very small to pretty large. I love turtles. As we passed them, I remembered the time Tommy caught a small turtle and let me hold it as he took a picture. We pretended I caught it. We both knew the truth.

At various places along the river, we took pictures with the beautiful cypress trees as the background. Sometimes we were lucky and able to include an ibis or egret in the picture. We also shot a video of the scenery we passed, the birds on the sides and in the air, and the river before us. We wanted Rick to get the whole experience as he viewed the video when we had our weekend party this weekend.

It was serene along the river. Sometimes I thought of Ohio and was so happy to be in Florida – where I thought I could never have the happy life I had in Ohio. The truth was I never had a happier life than in Florida with family and Tommy.

'Time for lunch,' I said and passed him a PB & J.

'My favorite,' he said with a smile.

'I know. I also brought orange juice and granola bars.'

We snacked as the kayaks floated downstream.

Then, suddenly, in front of us was a huge gator climbing out of the water, chomping on something – his lunch I supposed. I was terrified. It was a narrow section of the river and I never like being that up close and personal with a wild animal that could eat me and never think twice. 'I don't think I can go by that thing. It's too close,' I finally said.

'Just float on by. He won't bother with us,' Tommy reassured.

'How can you be so sure? We hear stories all the time,' I said.

'Not today. It's too perfect of a day. We'll be okay,' he said as we floated by.

When we passed that gator, it was eerie. He stopped chomping for a moment, turned his massive head my way, and then turned it back facing forward and went back to chomping. We floated by and soon after I stopped shaking.

After about three miles down the five-mile run, we spotted monkeys. 'There they are,' Tommy said.

'Get the bananas,' I kindly ordered.

'Got 'em right here,' he said as he held up the bananas.

To stay near the monkeys, we had to latch onto overhanging branches because the current is strong all along the river. If we didn't hang onto the branches, we would continue to float down river and we'd miss the monkey encounter.

All the monkeys want a banana. They come swinging through the trees and calling their monkey chatter. To get them the bananas, we put them on the end of the paddle and held the paddle in their direction. They don't like water, so they climb out on the branches as far as they can safely and retrieve the fruit. Then, they have to run away and eat them quickly or one of the others will take it from them. I always wish we had one for every monkey but there are too many of them.

Eventually, we make it to the end of the run. We turn to the left off the main river and head to the take-out. I always said how much I liked when something started and was sad when it ended. This was no different.

'Our fun always seems to go so fast,' I said with a hint of sadness in my voice.

'I know, but we'll do it again and again!' he exclaimed. He meant it too.

We took the kayaks out and I loaded mine into the transport hanger and road back to retrieve my truck. I picked Tommy up and we drove home. He was still in 'happy' mode and talked the whole way home. I listened.

3

Michael

It was back to work the next day and it was sure busy. We had one emergency after another to deal with. I was just catching up when I was asked to see Bella, a dog that ingested sugar-free gum. Xylitol is the sugar in that gum and, while it's safe for humans, it's unsafe for dogs. Dogs' blood sugar drops to dangerously low levels. This beautiful Golden Retriever ingested a considerable amount of the sugar-free gum and was now unconscious and I knew there was a chance of seizures due to the ingestion of the gum.

The owner said, 'Bella vomited before losing consciousness and there was a small amount of the ingested gum in the vomit.'

'We'll take good care of her,' I said reassuringly.

The team and I worked very quickly to obtain blood to test for a glucose (sugar) level. The level was 38 mg/%. This is how sugar levels are measured in human and animal blood. It means there are 38 milligrams of glucose (sugar) in 100 milliliters of blood.

This 38mg/% is dangerously low and pets can be lost if not treated. Normal sugar levels should be over 70 or 80 mg/%. Low blood sugar levels cause the symptoms we were seeing and high levels indicate the pet has diabetes mellitus - a disease where the body cannot process sugar properly and the pet usually does not have sufficient insulin in their body. Insulin is a hormone made in the pancreas that allows sugar to leave the blood and enter the cells of the body so they can do their work.

We placed an intravenous catheter and gave her a syringe full of 50% dextrose. This solution has a large amount of this sugar and raised Bella's blood sugar immediately. I was happy when she opened her eyes and lifted her head. 'Hello, gorgeous,' I said to her. 'It's good to see you responding.'

We weren't out of the woods though. The infusion of the sugar into her veins only helps temporarily. She was deemed a critical care patient because she needed constant monitoring and treatment as indicated for her dropping blood sugar levels until she processed all the xylitol. She ingested the artificial sugar too long before care for us to induce vomiting to rid her of the xylitol. So, we had to monitor her as she eliminated the xylitol.

The team is great at caring for critical pets.

They took frequent blood sugars, ran an intravenous drip with 5% dextrose (sugar) in the bag, and watched her for any change in her status. She recovered in a few hours and her blood sugar was stable without any further treatment. Thankfully, Bella went home to be a stinker with her owners for more years to come and instructions that included, 'No more sugar-free gum!'

In the middle of the chaos, Michael called. He wanted to do lunch. I told him how busy the day was and he insisted I take a break. If for nothing else, to clear my head and decompress.

I decided to join him after seeing my last appointment - a little Shar-Pei puppy in for her last boosters. Boy are those little things cute when they're pups. They have the softest skin and those wrinkles are beyond words. We kiss and kiss and kiss those little ones every time they come in to see us. Little Valentina is no exception. She took her vaccines like a champ and all is well.

Michael arrived a little early and, as a result, had to sit in the waiting room until I finished. He never seemed to mind. I think he could strike up a conversation with a mannequin. As a matter of fact, I think he has. He talked to an elderly gentleman with a poodle. They talked about younger days and where the man adopted his little dog.

'Hey, how are you?' I asked with a slight hint of *I'm having a very difficult day* tone in my voice.

'Great! Looking forward to lunch with you,'

he said with a big smile on his face. 'You need a break. I can tell.'

I could always count on Michael to cheer me up. He supported everything I did and do.

'Where'd you have in mind?' I asked.

'I'll leave that up to you; my treat wherever you pick.'

'Well,' I began, 'how about a little diner just up the street? Homemade cooking and small atmosphere.'

'Sounds great.'

Michael knew how I loved mom-and-pop restaurants and quiet as much as possible. Once he took me to a steak house where the music was so loud we couldn't even hear each other talking. I think we were both glad to get out of there.

'How's work?' he asked.

'It's been busy today. Lots of emergencies as well as routine appointments. I have surgery to do when I get back. The dog has a huge cut on his leg I need to sew closed. The staff is starting antibiotics and gave sedation medications.'

He drove to the restaurant as I looked around at the stores I pass every day but can't turn my head to see them. We drove into the parking lot and he opened my car door and the restaurant door for me. 'To what do I owe this royal treatment?' I asked.

'Just being a gentleman,' he replied.

Just as I loved; there were many customers, but there was a small restaurant feel and homemade pies lined the glass case near the front. Seating was available and we were escorted to ours by a bubbly hostess who did her job well.

After we ordered, Michael asked, 'What have you been up to lately?'

'I went kayaking with Tommy over the weekend.'

'You did?' His voice sounded a bit puzzled.

'Yes. Why? Something wrong?' I asked as I arranged my silverware and glass of water to make room for my meal.

'Well, did you have a nice time?'

'Very nice. The weather was perfect. The water was clear and we saw turtles, cranes, kites – which Tommy always likes to point out how they have a V-shaped tail – and we were lucky enough to see the monkeys. There weren't many others on the river, so we felt like we had the place to ourselves. It was nice to get away to nature for a few hours.'

I continued telling him about seeing the gator on the log chomping and he cringed. I told him about giving bananas to the monkeys and having peanut butter and jelly sandwiches.

'Oh, yeah. Love those peanut butter and jelly sandwiches,' he said as he rolled his eyes.

'We like 'em. Tommy packs them every time he packs, so I did this time.'

Michael didn't say anything, but he had a puzzled look about him. I ignored it as the server brought our sandwiches.

'Thank you,' I said as she placed the plate in front of me. Then, I turned to Michael and said, 'Hey, I was thinking, do you have time to walk the refuge with me? I won't go by myself. It scares me to be alone in isolated areas.'

'Sure. I would love to take a walk with you. When?' Michael asked. His face was normal this time.

'I was thinking this weekend? You're not working and I have the morning off.'

'Sounds like a plan. Will Tommy be joining us?' he half laughed.

'I don't think so, but I can ask him if you want me to.'

I didn't look up at him this time. I was busy finishing my delicious corned beef sandwich and fries. It was a nice treat for me because I was the only one at my house that likes corned beef. They all prefer roast beef, but I like both. My mother says I'll eat anything and I think that's almost true. I had some ground turkey the other day that wasn't the greatest.

'It's up to you,' Michael said a little slowly.

I knew Michael was sweet on me so I usually didn't talk about Tommy with him. He knew Tommy and I were just friends and that Tommy wasn't well, so he usually just spent time with me when I wasn't busy with Tommy. Sometimes we made plans like we just did for a walk.

'Well, this was super nice. Thanks for lunch and thanks for the break. I need to get back and care for the dog with the cut, finish the appointments, and head home. Tommy asked me to come over tonight and watch Jeopardy with him.'

'You're most welcome. It's always a pleasure to see you. Do you want to call me about the walk?'

'Yeah. I'll call you tomorrow and we can finish making plans.'

We drove back to the clinic, he gave me a peck on the cheek, and drove away. I watched him for a little while. I remembered the first time I met Michael. We were both working at the hospital where I was a nurse. He was with the ambulance team that brought my patients to me.

'I heard you're a Jesus freak?' he said sort of like a question, sort of like a statement.

Not knowing him at all and, since I was not sure what to say, I started, 'Well, I don't think I'm a freak, but I do love Jesus.'

'That's interesting.'

'How about you?' I boldly asked.

'Well, I'm Catholic. I coach a track team for one of the local churches.'

'Very nice.'

'The kids drive me crazy, but I love coaching.'

'How long have you been doing that?'

As I stood remembering, the only other thing I could remember is that he liked talking to me and he did every time he brought a patient into the emergency department where I worked even if the patient wasn't assigned to me.

4

The Refuge

That weekend Michael and I met at the Lake Woodruff Refuge. The refuge is close to my mother's home in Deleon Springs – named for the famous explorer, Ponce Deleon who discovered the *fountains of youth*. These are springs where a reported nineteen million gallons of water flows up from the ground into the spring area that feeds into 'runs' that feed into rivers and eventually to the ocean.

But, back to the refuge. Lake Woodruff is home to about 1500 gators, storks, hawks, owls, eagles, otters, kestrels, raccoons, sandhill cranes, and more. I have so many memories of walks here, but the one I will never forget is during one walk with my mum. We were walking along the path and, when I heard something and turned around, I saw a family of sandhill cranes coming our way. They weren't afraid of us because they've always been around the many people who come to the refuge.

As they approached, I wished I had my camera – it was a *Kodak moment* for sure. The mom sandhill crane was on one side of the lane, the dad on the other, and the little yellow baby sandhill crane strolled along in the middle of these parents. It was precious and priceless. And, no camera.

There was always something new and wonderful to experience each time I walked this refuge. I was looking forward to what we would see today.

'This is nice. How do you know about this refuge?' Michael asked as he stepped out of his car.

'My mum brought me here when I first came to Florida. It's been a quiet place to enjoy time away from the city and lots of folks.'

'It is spectacular,' he commented.

'Well, we have two choices. We can take a short walk that cuts out about halfway down this long path,' I said as we looked down the half-mile path in front of us, 'or we can walk the whole way. What are you up for?'

Michael looked down the long, long lane and finally said, 'Let's do the whole walk.'

'Great!' And off we went.

The sun was high and there was just a slight breeze that made the hot days in Florida just a little more bearable. I wouldn't trade the warmth, though, for the cold I left behind in Ohio.

The first thing we saw as we started down

the lane was a small gator in a ditch that runs along the path. 'Oh, look at the eyes staring up at us,' I said.

'I dare you to jump down there and catch him. He's small,' Michael challenged.

'Never! No way!' I snapped. 'You never know if there's a big one close by them. They are sneaky and hard to see sometimes.'

We laughed and continued walking. A little further down the path, I pointed and said, 'Look, otters are playing in the pond there.'

Michael glanced in the direction of my finger and we both walked closer to the pond to watch the little heads bob up and down out of and into the water. Then, they darted at lightning speed from one side of the pond to the other. The one chased the other. So cute. I'm such a girl.

'So, you said you spent time on the river with Tommy the other day,' Michael started to say.

'We do lots of things despite his health,' I interrupted.

'Yeah. About that. What's he dealing with, if you don't mind my asking?'

'He has so many things going on. He had open heart surgery several years ago so he's on a blood thinner. He had his knee replaced also, but that doesn't seem to be a problem for him. I think the most difficult thing for him is his lungs. He has a hard time breathing. He has lupus and that attacks different areas of different people's bodies. His lupus is attacking his lungs.'

'How sick is he?'

'He's been told he will die. It really upsets me that the doctors basically tell him to stop at the store on the way home and pick up a shovel. They aren't that bad, but just about. I mean *every time* he goes to the doctor, they say the same thing. He's not curable, he's going to die. I can see the sadness in his eyes sometimes and he told Rick he's afraid.'

'Afraid to die?'

'That and getting weaker. When I first came, Tommy was able to walk four miles and swim in the deep side of the spring pool. Then, he started taking shorter walks around the local grocery store close to his apartment. He counts how many times he manages to walk around the complex. Sometimes he walks only once around the store and sometimes he does five 'laps' he called it. At the spring, he changed his program up some and now he swims in the shallower section because if he gets tired, he needs to be able to stand in the water so he doesn't drown.'

'Sounds serious.'

'Oh, yes. It is.'

Suddenly, I shouted as I looked to the sky, 'Look! There's a kestrel.' Michael's eyes followed mine.

Once, when I walked the refuge with Tommy, we saw a kestrel. Tommy knew what it was immediately and taught me something new that day. Kestrels are predatory birds in the falcon family. They're small but incredibly beautiful. I never saw one 'til I came to Florida. I told Michael all about that walk.

'He's pretty smart,' Michael said as half a question and half a statement. 'So, back to Tommy's health. Are the doctors right? Is he close to dying?'

'Yes, I guess. I see the way he breathes and sometimes he struggles so badly I don't think he's going to make it to the car. I took him to his doctor's appointment one day and he couldn't walk back to where I parked my truck, so he stayed near the entrance door and I went for the truck. When I came to pick him up, he was looking off into the distance and all I could feel was sorrow because the look on his face seemed hopeless and sad. It made me very sad.'

I stopped for a moment, tried to hold back the tears, and then continued, 'I want to call the doctors and beg them to *stop* telling him he's so sick. I want them to tell him he's doing pretty darn good for someone who has his struggles. I just don't think doctors and others should take away someone's hope. I think Tommy should live without fear as much as possible and when they tell him the *cold, hard facts*, it really rains on his parade.'

We walked in silence for a short while enjoying the scenery. The refuge had plenty to see. There were tall palm trees and flowers scattered everywhere. Pink hollyhocks were my very favorite and were in bloom everywhere along the path. Little yellow flowers that resembled buttercups were in bloom today as well. There were overgrown grasses and cattails all around the ditches created to help stop the 'swamp effect' Florida was famous for at one time.

I broke the silence, 'I know the future is grim. Once we went to the Keys and Tommy slept in his van while I slept in a tent. I woke earlier than he and sat by the gulf side of the ocean admiring the view while he slept in. I remember praying and asking for more time for Tommy. When I heard him rustling in the van, I was standing there when he opened the side door and sat up. I smiled and said, 'It's a great day for Key Lime pie!' He looked at me and called me his *Miss Sunshine*. I wish I could have helped him more. I just didn't want him to know I was scared too. Scared of losing him and scared of what to do with my life when I lost him because he consumed my every moment really.'

'It's sad and happy to spend time with someone who has a limited time, isn't it?' Michael stated.

'Yes. It's heart-breaking actually. We have had so many good memories together and I cherish each and every one of them.'

'What do you think you'll feel when he does pass?' Michael asked tenderly.

'I'm not sure. I try not to think about it too much. I try to just be in the moment. I must admit I think about what it will be like when we lose him. For the most part, my whole life is being at his beck and call.'

'How do you mean?'

'Well, I wait for his calls and we make plans. Like the other day when we went to the river. We don't go to the ocean anymore, but we went years ago and it was so much fun. He would throw me into the waves while I was riding an inner tube. He did it over and over and the waves were huge on the ocean the day we were there. Now, I wait for anything he wants to do. Sometimes we go on the river and sometimes I pick up a pizza and movies from the library and we have a day where we veg out and watch one movie after another. I wash his clothes and he hands me his shopping list and I do his shopping. I know him so well I never get anything wrong. And, when I bring in the jars of lemonade, I sneak and take the seal off the mouth of each bottle. I have to be careful because he's very independent and likes to do as much for himself as he can. Once he caught me taking the seals off and said, 'I forgot to thank you for that. Those are hard for me to get off.' I smiled because I wanted to be helpful without him feeling badly.'

'Sounds like you spend a lot of time with him.'

'I do. We've been friends forever and, when I came to Florida, he sort of took over my time. He just assumes he can call anytime and we'll do things as he's able. He called this morning and asked me to come over tonight and watch Jeopardy with him. He said he had some other things he had to do this morning, so he couldn't come walk with us.'

As we made the turn around the long stretch of the path around the refuge, we stopped suddenly. 'It's a wood stork,' I said before I realized Michael already knew that.

'I know,' Michael replied. 'Did you forget how much I know about birds?'

I didn't answer that but said, 'You know what I find so funny about wood storks? It's how they look like they've had a really rough night.'

'I see it,' Michael said and we both laughed.

'You love birding don't you?' I asked.

'I do. They're so interesting to me. I've been studying them for the longest time.'

Michael dazzled me with his knowledge of birds for the next fifteen minutes of our walk. He knew all about grouse and hummingbirds and the migration of some interesting birds.

'It's nice to have something that allows you to enjoy nature as much as you have with the birds,' I stated. 'I wish I knew more about them. Once I heard a little bird migrates an outrageous distance each year - something like five thousand miles. The little bird knows the way.'

Michael smiled. He did know that. 'Would you like to continue our lively banter over dinner?' he asked.

'I would love to but I have those plans with Tommy.'

5

Jeopardy Nights

That evening, I arrived at Tommy's apartment just in time for Jeopardy. I really enjoyed spending evenings with Tommy. It was relaxing and I was always amazed at how many questions to the answers Tommy knew. I usually knew two or three but I didn't even say those out loud because I knew it was important to Tommy to feel he was smart. He was, of course. I was smart too, but not at Jeopardy. I never wanted to make anything a competition between us.

I did well with the science and medicine categories in Jeopardy, but forget geography and history and art and many other categories. The truth is I don't even know where New Hampshire is in relation to Maine. In addition, art and Shakespeare were not my categories either. Today, one of the contestants was minus two hundred dollars when it was time for Final Jeopardy. They weren't permitted to compete in Final Jeopardy with a negative score. I thought, '*That would be me.*'

'Are you off tomorrow?' Tommy asked when the program was over.

'Yes. I talked to Rick and he wants to do a movie and lunch or a walk in Flagler Beach and lunch in the park.'

'What do you want to do?' he asked.

'Doesn't matter to me. What about you?'

'What movie's playing?'

'I looked at the listings, but there wasn't anything I thought we'd want to see. Since we went to the movies last week, how about we go for a walk on the walking path near the river?'

'That's what I was hoping you wanted to do,' he said. 'How about you pick me up and we drive to get the van?'

'Perfect,' I said.

Tommy was having a little more difficulty breathing today. His sentences were broken and his chest heaved up and down as he tried to talk. When he excused himself to the men's room and returned, he couldn't catch his breath for two or three minutes. He must have seen the worried look on my face because he said, 'Don't feel bad, I would feel bad if this was happening to someone I love.'

'Well, it is happening to someone I love and I am worried,' I said with a tone in my voice that made him know I meant it.

'You know, I was thinking....'

Tommy was always thinking, so I braced

myself for a little talk time. Some talks I wish we didn't have to have. I knew he was lonely and I spent far too much time at work. I frequently wished I would quick work and spend all my time with him. The time I did spend never seemed like it was enough.

'I think if people really knew, really, really knew, what heaven is like, they would want to go there now and not be here. I think they would end their lives just to go there. I think that's why we aren't able to know that while we're here,' he said seriously. 'I think there's a little doubt in all of us. Is it really real? What if there's nothing? What will it all be like? Just so we don't want to go.'

I've been singing songs about heaven for many years and can see how I've talked frivolously about it to others for many years. Death always seemed like something we talked about in the *Sweet By and By* but was never really real. Here was a man facing the end of his life and I really didn't know what to say and I never peddle easy answers to difficult questions.

'I never thought of that. I agree we don't know exactly what it'll be like and, in fact, sometimes I find myself wondering just what *it will* be like. I only know life here on earth and the things we go through here. The Bible says there will be no more pain or suffering. We finally don't cry anymore or hurt in any way. Sounds like the place everyone would want to be; and want to be now.'

'I know. We've lost so many people we

know.' He paused for a moment and looked down. Then he said, 'I want you to know I feel like I could die any day.'

These words hit me like someone just hit me with a baseball bat. They made me incredibly sad. So sad that I wasn't sure what to say. Then, I put on my brave face, smiled as large as I could, and said, 'Well, not today, dear friend. Not today.' It's difficult to think of something meaningful to say at a time like this. It's easy to give stupid responses but that's not what I wanted to do.

'I have a lot of things wrong with me that you don't know,' he continued.

'That's why I'm here,' I said, nonchalantly, as I moved my gaze to the ceiling.

Tommy seemed stunned. He didn't say anything. He wasn't expecting me to say that and was so taken by surprise he was speechless. That didn't happen very often. I think he was trying to figure out what I meant. Apparently, he didn't realize why I uprooted my life and left my home and friends to help him and be with him as much as I could.

'Did you walk today?' I asked, trying to lighten the conversation.

'Yes. But I only walked in the apartment. My breathing wasn't good today, so I went from here to the bathroom.'

Tommy pointed to where he was sitting in the living room of his apartment and showed me a small cut-off piece of paper he put tally marks –

also called hash marks - to count his trips to the bathroom and back; a distance of about twenty feet. I only saw the paper for a split second, but there were at least thirty marks. He pushed himself all the time. Some days he felt great and some days he felt sick and that discouraged him. That's why I wished the doctors would tell him he was doing great. What harm would it have done to tell him this? In fact, I think it would have helped him feel better for more days. Hope is always a good thing. The way we think matters when it comes to our health and well-being. I'm convinced of it.

'What are you working next week?' Tommy asked. He seemed to want to change the subject and I was grateful.

'I'm off Tuesday and Wednesday. Want to do a bike ride?'

'Yeah. I was thinking we could ride in Deland behind the police station. That's close. Then, we can get some movies from the library and cook here.'

'Sounds like a plan.'

I would cook is what he meant. Tommy only knew how to make spaghetti and television dinners. He was so easy to cook for because he craved homemade food and even mine was a treat for him. I either picked up rice, vegetables, and meat to make stir fry or I chose sausages to make sausage sandwiches on hoagie buns with onions and peppers and red sauce. It was nice to see him eat and ask for seconds!

We watched television in silence for a few minutes. My mind drifted to one of our past bicycle rides. Tommy had a racing bike that was so light he could lift it with two fingers. That was great for him because anything strenuous caused him to have difficulty breathing. We took the bikes to a remote area a few miles from his apartment. He said he loved the homes in the neighborhood and wanted me to see them.

The homes were truly spectacular. Some were huge and had several sections to them and two or three levels; or stories. I noticed that most homes in Florida only had one level. I always assumed it was due to the hurricanes in this state. Homes also didn't have basements and I did know this is because of the high water table here.

When we passed by some of the homes, Tommy described them perfectly. I could tell he'd been past them before and knew which ones he wanted to show me. I wondered if he would like a home. He never said and I didn't ask.

This reminded me of the Bible where Jesus tells us that *In His Father's house, there are many mansions. Jesus goes to prepare a place for us...* This always makes me smile when I think someone like my friend – who couldn't afford a home or had the health to care for a home here – will have a mansion in heaven. I sure hope it's a nice and big one; like the homes he showed me here. I think Tommy will really like his.

It was difficult to talk about death with

Tommy because I knew he didn't *want* to die. I know that sounds strange, but he loved life and lived it to the fullest. He enjoyed people and the rivers and movies and lunches and bicycle rides and walks and more. Others I knew who were given sad news by doctors felt the same way.

Some friends I knew said they were ready to go to heaven and had prayed to go. One friend, Steve, was a paralyzed man whose wife cared for him for over thirty-five years. He had pneumonia again and was tired. He wanted to go *home*. His wife cried and begged him to want to live and, when he finally convinced her to let him go, she talked about his mansion waiting for him. Then, she asked, '*Who do you want to see first when you get there?*' To which he responded, '*You.*' She wasn't going quite yet, but I think Jesus is okay with this request. He knew how much Steve loved and appreciated the woman who lovingly cared for him for so many years.

I was lost in my thoughts about what it would be like to receive life-altering news and facing what I truly believe about God and heaven and all those that we had said '*goodbye*' to when I remembered how Tommy had to stop to catch his breath on that bike ride.

We stopped in the middle of a sidewalk on a busy street. A woman noticed Tommy and, with concern in her voice, asked, 'Do you need help?'

She was unable to see me, so I moved forward, waved my arm, and said, 'We're good.

Thank you very much.'

She went about her business as I stayed with Tommy until he was ready to ride again. I was always protecting him as best I could. He couldn't talk in that situation and it was embarrassing for him to even be in that situation, but he bravely went out and did things anyway. Even if it meant people would see him struggling to breathe.

Suddenly, my thoughts were back in the apartment as Tommy said, 'So, you'll pick me up tomorrow?'

'Sure will.'

'Great. I'll pack turkey sandwiches with mayonnaise and I have some snack cakes and soda for us for lunch.'

'Sounds great,' I said. 'Do you think I should stay with you now? I don't think you should be alone.'

'No. I'll be alright.'

When I got home, my dad asked where I was all evening.

'At Tommy's,' I replied.

He looked puzzled but didn't comment.

6

Rick's Day Out

Rick was injured in a motorcycle accident that left him paralyzed from the neck down. He lived with my sister for seven years after his accident but now lived in a surprisingly nice veteran's nursing home in Daytona Beach.

It would be years before I appreciated the love my sister had for him and the sacrifices she made to care for him. A *total care* patient can be exhausting. You are everything to them. They cannot prepare their own food and most cannot retrieve beverages for themselves. In addition, most cannot even do simple things like scratch their noses. Rick had some mobility, but it was limited.

My sister is a nurse and a very good one, to be honest. She is meticulous in her care for her patients and Rick was no exception. She did exercises, personal care, took him to movies with just the two of them or all of us, walked the Daytona boardwalk frequently and watched fireworks, fed him well, took him to concerts and doings at the Ocean Center in Daytona, and more. Once they invited me to see Kenny G with them. Fabulous concert.

My sister was devoted to making Rick feel like he was the most important person in the world. She knew who would make him feel special and where he would be treated specially, so she made sure that's where they went much of the time.

The truth was, we all loved Rick like he was always part of our family and that meant a lot to him. When we talked *real talk*, he shared many things that made me think he spent the majority of his life looking for somewhere to belong; somethings or *some ones* to give him meaning.

Now he has us and Tommy was committed to making sure we included him any time we could. For lots of reasons, Rick couldn't come on the river with us, but everything he could do, we did together. That's where the video camera came in handy. When Tommy and I did something fun – whether kayaking the river or going to the Keys – we took the video with us so we could show the highlights to Rick.

Sometimes I forgot to think about how it must feel to be in a wheelchair. I take so many things for granted. Rick never complained and he was always in a cheery mood. He said one of the only pleasures he had was to eat and, since there felt like there was so little I could do to make his life better, I sent him lunches from different restaurants every other day. He enjoyed the sushi, the oysters, the chicken, the Chinese, the other seafood, and more. If he asked for something specific, I sent it along with all my love.

Once, Rick was extremely ill. I thought he was going to die. I asked him, 'Are you ready to go to heaven.'

He smiled at me and weakly said, 'Well, at least I would be able to walk again.'

I cried inside. There were so many days he never said anything, and I didn't always think about it, but deep down inside, I knew. He watched us all swim in the ocean he loved and he watched us ride bicycles and me on a horse and he sat. He took videos of all of us so he could bless us with memories and have something he could watch over and over to remember the good times we spent together.

Before Rick was injured, he was a skydiver and a pilot. He said he wanted to touch the sky. I, however, am a big chicken and never want to touch the sky. Even flying makes me nervous, but I do it anyway.

Rick and I decided to write a children's book together. Rick added the rescue of a down skydiver in Norway to the special book he helped write. Rick considered himself blessed to have a *second chance* at everything after an accident that should have, could have, claimed his life. *In Search of Christmas* was awarded a Purple Dragon WINNER award.

Rick had the mindset that there's always

something fun to do no matter the circumstances in life. For the most part, I knew Rick appreciated a second chance at life and loved life despite being in a wheelchair. I often heard others comment that he would be better off had he not survived the accident, but Rick didn't feel that way. Our love made life worth everything to him. He said so.

And now, Tommy was committed to making sure we spent time with him. Tommy said, 'I just want to make his life better.' Tommy did make peoples' lives better. He made my life better and he made Rick's life better.

Today, the trip Tommy and I planned to share with Rick was to drive to a nice park near the inter-coastal waterway in Dayona Beach. I understand this waterway stretches up the entire east coast of our country. The walking path there runs right along the water and the boats putter by. We are also blessed with the enchanting nature that Florida nicely provides each time we step out into it. There's a special park to enjoy our packed lunch as well.

My sister owns a handicap-accessible van, so when we wanted to go somewhere, we just booked the date with her – ha ha. She left the keys on the tire when she was away. I retrieved the van and set off for the nursing home.

At the nursing home, I signed Rick out for the day and went to his room. He was already in his electric wheelchair. 'You're all signed out. Ready?' I asked.

'I just need my meds.'

He wheeled out, we found his nurse, he took his meds, and off we went to the van. I was so scared the first time I used that lift. I didn't want to take him anywhere because I was afraid of the lift. I just knew he would roll off the thing and crash to his death in front of me. I also worried the support the lift was attached to would break off the van and he would tumble to a severe injury or death. These things never happened, thank goodness. But, every time I had to use the lift, I was anxious until he was on or off the lift.

I opened the back doors, electronically unfolded the lift out of the van, and moved it down to the street. Rick rolled onto the lift like a pro, I pressed the buttons to make the lift rise to the level of the van floor, open, and allow him to wheel off the lift into the van. *Phew!* I said to myself. We made it again.

I folded the lift up again, closed the back doors, locked him in, put his seat belt on, and jumped into the driver's seat.

Rick sat behind my seat a little to the middle so he could see the road. He was a real *backseat driver* and never missed a mistake I made. He made comments about my changing lanes in an intersection, not using my turn signal, and more. To be honest, I never knew we weren't allowed to change lanes in an intersection. Sometimes it's the best time to make my move.

'Just watch that tablet of yours, Rick, and let

me do the driving,' I'd say.

'Just doin' my job, ma'am,' he'd say with a crooked smile on his face and a poorly executed southern accent. Since he was a pilot, I called him my *wingman*. I know that has other meanings, but for us, it meant he was my right-hand man.

We always managed to have fun when we all spent time together. When I first came to Florida, the whole gang did things. We went to the ocean a few times a week and rode the waves as we hopped on boogie boards, we had lunch at various beach restaurants, shopped – my personal favorite, visited museums, and everyone took me to fun cities like St. Augustine.

'Where're we going today?' Rick asked.

'Tommy wants to go to the walking path by the river because it'll be easy for your chair there. Then, we want to have lunch over in the park.'

'Tommy?' Rick asked, puzzled.

'Yeah, he wanted you to have a day out with us.'

'How could he be here? Where is he?'

I didn't answer him at first because I was busy getting settled in my driver's chair and slipping into my seatbelt.

Tommy had a little trouble but managed to climb into the passenger seat.

'Ready,' he said.

'Ready, Rick?' I said as I looked in the rearview mirror.

'Let's do it!' he exclaimed. 'How about a

little music on the radio?'

'I can do that,' I said. Tommy picked a CD and I put it in the slot.

Away we went to *Homeward Bound* and *Bridge Over Troubled Waters* by Simon and Garfunkel.

I pulled the van out of the nursing home drive and we headed for the coast. We had little traffic and Rick spent time on his tablet. I guess he was used to passing time that way.

'It's a great day for a walk,' Tommy said.

'Sure is,' I replied.

'Sure is, what?' Rick asked.

'A nice day,' I said.

'Yeah, it sure is. Don't miss the weather in the North, do you?' Rick said in the form of a question.

'Not a bit,' I answered. 'I miss home sometimes, but not the weather.'

'It's paradise here in the winter,' Tommy commented.

'That it is,' I responded.

'That it is, what?' Rick asked. He seemed puzzled.

'It's a paradise in the winter,' I said in an annoyed tone. Didn't he hear Tommy?

'Sure is,' Rick replied.

We finally arrived at our destination. Tommy said, 'I'm going to the men's room while you unload Rick.'

'Sure.'

I unbuckled my belt, headed for the back of the van, unbelted Rick, took off the chair restraints, and headed for the back doors as he turned himself around to get to the lift. Getting him out of the van was the opposite procedure as getting him into the van. It was still anxiety-producing because his chair weighs over six hundred pounds and he's a little over two hundred pounds, so that lift has a lot of work to do.

While I was unloading Rick from the van, he had a concerned look on his face and asked, 'Hey, can I ask you something?'

'Sure,' I said.

'Who are you talking to when you're not talking to me?'

'Tommy,' I snapped impatiently. How could he ask such a question?

'How can you be talking to Tommy?' he asked.

'I don't know what you mean. He organized our whole day off. Stop kidding around,' I said and ignored him. He proceeded to roll off the lift once it was lowered to the ground.

Out we were!!! 'Ready?' I asked both men as Tommy joined us.

'Yes, let's go,' Rick said.

We all started on the paved path. We walked for a short while and then came to a little creek with a wooden bridge. Tommy always liked to stop and look for fish and birds that might be hanging around. I suspected his breathing needed a break.

Tommy was unable to talk when he walked, so he was silent. But he was able to talk when he rested for a moment.

'There's a small ibis on the bank of the creek,' Tommy said, pointing.

'See the birds, Rick?' I asked and pointed.

'Yes. They're great.'

We continued on and through the woods, past houses, and along the river. The sun was high in the cloudless blue sky and, before we knew it, it was pretty warm. The path was shaded, so we weren't worried about Rick overheating, but we always kept this in mind.

Cyclists whizzed by, walkers going the opposite way greeted us cheerfully, Tommy took frequent rest stops, and we occasionally took a few minutes to watch the fishermen on the bank of the inter-coastal fishing. It was relaxing and nice to have a day off work.

After we walked for about twenty-five minutes, I asked, 'It's twenty-five minutes back, do you think we should turn around?'

'Sure,' both men said. We all turned and headed back to the van.

I loaded Rick in the van and we were off to the park for lunch. YUM.

There were a few people there, but it was a weekday, so most people worked as we enjoyed ourselves. I parked in a shady spot and helped Rick off the van and then helped Tommy with lunch. If I set Rick up, he was able to eat himself. He has a specially bent fork that he stabs the food with and is able to use his shoulders to lift his arm so his hand can manage to get the food to his mouth.

I cut up the turkey and mayonnaise sandwich, put a straw in the large drinking glass filled with lemonade, and set these, along with a small bowl of strawberries and grapes, on his chair tray. He went to work on lunch as Tommy and I helped ourselves to food.

I always loved this park because there's a boardwalk in one section with so many turtles I can't count them and small alligators. The small alligators don't frighten me, just the big ones do; for obvious reasons.

We spent some time throwing our leftover bread into the water for the turtles and enjoyed just a few more minutes of our lovely Florida weather before we headed back to the nursing home where I kissed Rick *goodbye* for the hundredth time and told him I'd order him some lunch the next day and see him again soon.

Another great day filled with memories. I smiled as I drove the van back to my sister's home and Tommy and I went home ourselves. He was tired, so we made it a short day.

7

Olivia and Dinner With Michael

It was another crazy day at the office. First thing after I arrived, Olivia, a 3-year-old Labradoodle, presented having trouble delivering her puppies. We call this dystocia.

According to all of our calculations, Olivia has been looking forward to having puppies for sixty-five days; two days past the usual sixty-three days a dog is pregnant. Miscalculations of days have been known to happen but, in any event, we were very close to the correct calculation of time and two days usually don't make a huge difference.

I asked the staff to take a few radiographs of Olivia's abdomen. We counted ten puppies in the films we refer to as 'pictures.' Sometimes pups are difficult to see because they're tucked behind each other or are hidden behind organs in the mama dog's abdomen.

What I do is look for the little heads attached to the spines to, hopefully, arrive at a correct puppy count. This is important because we want to know how many pups there are and if they appear to be healthy on the films. I didn't see any signs of abnormalities, including air around the pups which might indicate a problem with one of the pups.

Olivia has been restless all night. Her owners are concerned because she hasn't had any pups yet. We were concerned too. The decision to do a Cesarean section to remove the puppies was made. This surgery to deliver the pups is for emergencies like Olivia.

The staff prepared the operating room, placed an intravenous catheter in Olivia's front leg, completed some minor bloodwork, and I gathered the medication to anesthetize Olivia.

'We're almost ready for surgery. Do you all want to stay and wait here or run for a coffee or late breakfast?' I asked Olivia's owners.

'How long will this take?' the concerned owners asked.

'Once we get her to the surgery table, everything proceeds very quickly. We want to be quick to expose the pups to the least amount of anesthesia we can. They do better if we are quick,' I replied.

'Well, we'd like to stay close if that's ok?' they said.

'Sure,' I said reassuringly. 'We're great with whatever helps you get through all this. We can keep updated as we go along.'

As the staff completed the bloodwork, I finished up with a couple of other clients. One client was a Dachshund pup named Jack who was so cute I wanted to squeeze him. I vaccinated him for the major preventable diseases of dogs and gave him a general deworming medication.

I also examined a young Basset Hound with a slight ear infection. Those ears drag the ground on every Basset I have ever examined. But they sure are cute.

After finishing with my last few pets, I was called to the surgery table. All my staff was ready with dry towels to dry the pups and string to tie off their little umbilical cords. Here we go!!

I gave Olivia her sedation medication, intubated her, and placed her on the gas anesthesia machine. When she was completely anesthetized, I made my incision to open the skin. There was little fat under the skin, so I was able to see the 'white line' easily on the center of the abdominal muscles called the linea alba. There are no blood vessels here. This allows me to use my scalpel blade to make a long incision in this layer to open the abdomen without appreciable bleeding.

I must be extremely careful because, with ten pups inside it, Olivia's uterus is large and close to where I'm opening the abdomen. The uterus is so large I found it pressing against the abdominal wall as I made my initial incision.

Once inside, the large pregnant uterus is

easy to elevate from the abdomen. After I elevated the uterus and placed it on the sterile drape covering the abdomen, I carefully made my first incision into the uterus over one of the pups. Pups are wet and slimy and this makes them slippery. So, I always make sure I have a good grip on the pups as I deliver them from the uterus. Each pup is delivered separately, their umbilical cords are tied, and I hand off each pup to my staff.

Immediately, the staff takes the puppies in their dry towels and begin rubbing vigorously to dry them and stimulate breathing. I have the staff give each pup medication to reverse the anesthetic medication I used for Olivia that transfers to the pups before I remove them quickly enough. The anesthesia medication needs to be eliminated as quickly as possible because it delays the pups' breathing well, responding to us, and nursing with mom.

Yeah! The first pup is crying! This is a great sound in the delivery room. I proceed to gently milk the rest of the pups to my initial incision and remove them one by one. I hand each to the next staff member, and we repeat the process for all the pups.

Finally, we delivered all ten of the pups. Whew! It was good to be finished. All the pups are dry, crying, and doing well. Mom was also doing well. I proceeded to close my uterine incision, close Olivia's abdomen and skin, and wake her from anesthesia. The pups must be united with mom as soon as possible for bonding success as well as nursing mom's first special milk.

During a normal delivery, the mama dog receives the little one, removes the placenta and breaks the umbilical cord, cleans them, and allows them to begin nursing. Then, she looks for the next pup. This usually happens at a rate of one pup per thirty to sixty minutes. We hope a C-section delivers all the pups in less than ten minutes. So, it's easy to see how the rush goes in this situation and how all the pups need special attention for the first few minutes of their lives and then mom takes over. Thank the good Lord for this. Ten pups are a lot to handle, but mama dogs make it look like a piece of cake.

Ring! My phone rings as I remove my gloves. It's Michael. 'Hello.'

'Hey, how are you?' he asks.

'Just finished surgery. How are you?'

'What surgery?' Michael's always curious.

'C-section on a Labradoodle.'

'How'd it go?'

'She's great! She had ten lovely little pups. All are doing well. It's been a crazy morning.'

'Well, how about dinner tonight? Maybe a movie?'

'Can we do take-out and a movie in?' I asked. 'I'm pretty tired this week.'

'I can make that happen. How about six?'

'Sounds great. I'll call when I'm on the way.'

We hung up and I plopped in my chair in

front of my computer, opened my charting program, and caught up on paperwork. I guess it's still called *paperwork* even though there is no longer any paper. Guess I should call it *documenting*.

I typed my surgery notes and listed all the post-operative orders for Olivia and her pups. She was packed up and sent home where she'll continue to care for those little ones. We'll see all of them back in about five to seven weeks.

When I arrived home, Michael was waiting at the door with Chinese take-out and my favorite movie, *The Black Stallion Returns*. I have always loved Walter Farley's books about *The Black Stallion*. I pretended I was young Alec Ramsey who was shipwrecked at sea, traversed the ocean tied to a black horse, and landed on a deserted island. I also pretended I was the one who made friends with the wild stallion and rode him all over the island each day until rescued and returned home to America with my new horse! Then, in *The Black Stallion Returns*, a slightly older Alec has to cross the desert because the original owners of his black stallion have taken him from the lad. All great stuff and near-and-dear to my heart. I was consumed with reading every book as a young girl.

'Ah! You know just what makes me happy!' I shouted.

'I try.'

'Well, let me get into some comfy clothes while you put the movie in and get plates for the food.'

'Will do, Boss,' he said subserviently.

'That's not what I meant and you know it.' He smiled and started for the kitchen while I went to change.

We sat in the living room enjoying our food. About ten minutes into the movie, Michael asked, 'Have you seen Tommy lately?'

He had a look I can only describe as *suspicious* on his face as I answered, 'I saw him at the springs yesterday. He was practicing snorkeling for our upcoming trip to the Keys. Why do you ask?' And I looked *suspiciously* back at him.

'You're going to the Keys?' His tone was almost disbelief. It confuses me when he does this.

'Yes. We do every year,' I said matter-of-factly.

'When are you leaving?' His tone was much more sincere.

'Next week. I have time off work and we like the cooler weather. Although it's so far south, it's not really that cool.'

'Do you think he'd mind if I come along?'

'No. You want to come along?' I was puzzled.

'Well, I have never been to the Keys and you make it sound so wonderful.'

'It is. To be honest, Tommy would love a newbie to spew all his knowledge onto. He always has an agenda for us but, every time we meet someone along the way, he tells them all about his stories and adventures. Yeah, it would be nice to have you. Can you take time off to come?'

'Sure. That's why it's nice when you're your own boss.'

We finished the movie and were stuffed with Chinese food when Tommy showed me a picture of his brother, Murphy. I knew Murph because I was practically part of the family for years. He was one of Michael's two older brothers. Michael also had two sisters. Murphy was a smoker and, when I knew him later in life, he was on oxygen for lung disease. If there's one thing I learned after being in medicine for years is that things have a way of finally catching up with people.

'After we lost Murphy, I went through a pretty good bout of depression. Loss makes one think of one's own mortality. I didn't expect to miss him so much.'

'I know. It's a horribly awful feeling when you lose someone you're close to. Grief is different for everyone but I think everyone agrees that it's unpleasant for sure.'

'It was like a dark cloud around me. Something I couldn't shake. Sometimes I wanted to cry, but couldn't. Then, when I did cry, it was like a river. I saw everyone else happy and just couldn't crack a smile. I had no motivation and wanted to stay in bed all day. I didn't want to eat or bathe or see friends. I figured I feel better one day.'

'Sounds incredibly sad.'

'It was. There were times I felt Murph was

still with me and I could still hear his voice and think he wasn't really gone. I would have endless conversations with him. I'd discuss what I was having for dinner, as though he was still with me. As always, it made me feel he was reminding me to eat healthier.' We both chuckled.

'Wow,' I said. 'That's Murphy for you. You must miss him so much. I have such good memories of him too. He used to send me funny emails all the time and I laughed at all of them. I still have those emails. Sometimes I read them and look up to heaven and tell him I miss him and know he's breathing better now.'

'I do too. He told me you and he talked a lot. Like I was saying, after he passed, I would feel him so close. It was as if he never left. We laughed at silly things together – things we thought were funny and silly anyway....'

'I remember how we'd talk on the phone for hours,' I interrupted.

'Sometimes I would sit for long periods and feel him so close,' Michael continued. 'This went on for some time.'

'You mean you didn't think he left?'

'No. I knew he did. I just felt like I couldn't accept this and wanted him to be close and still here. Did you ever feel like this?'

'Me?' I said surprised by the question. 'I don't think so.' I was sort of stunned, not sure how to answer that. 'What do you mean? How did you realize Murphy wasn't with you anymore?'

'Well, gradually, I realized he died and knew he wanted me to be happy and continue living a good life until I would see him again in heaven.'

'I see.' But the truth was I didn't see what he was getting at at all. 'Why are you sharing this with me?'

'I just wanted to.'

'So, you don't talk to Murphy anymore?' I asked.

'I do in my prayers, but I know he's not here.'

'Well, that's good, I guess. It means you aren't hurting as much as you were, right?' I tried to be logical.

'Yes. That's what it means to me.'

I got up to clear the plates and said, 'Well, I had a great evening. Thanks for being willing to stay in tonight. Thanks for dinner and the movie. You know all my faves.'

'Yes, I do.' He smiled.

'So, I'll let you know about the Keys. Tommy won't mind at all. There's plenty of room for all of us.'

As he started to leave, Michael placed his hand on my shoulder and said, 'You do know how special you are to me and how much I care about you, right?'

His blue eyes were so sincere. I smiled and said matter-of-factly, 'I know. It means a great deal to me. Thank you.'

8

Heading to the Keys

We were traveling southbound, headed to the Florida Keys! It was a perfect day for the seven-hour drive. We left before sunrise this morning and, finally, the sun was starting to pop up.

'Time for the sunglasses,' I said as I reached toward the dash to find my fashionable sunglasses and put them on. There were several things I considered mandatory 'equipment' for anyone living in Florida. Sunglasses were one thing. And there was sunscreen, of course, a wetsuit, a mask, snorkel, and fins, water shoes, a kayak, swimsuits and other beach wear with towels, a bicycle, boogie boards, and last, but not least, flip-flops. Mom said she was going to get me a T-shirt that said, '*I wear flip-flops all year 'round*' because I do!

'Pretty nice day. That's for sure,' Michael said.

'I do love Florida. It's sunny most of the time. It feels strange when it rains for more than a short time and the clouds hide the sun.'

'Sure is a lot different than Ohio, huh?' he asked, already knowing the answer.

'Well, we're almost done with this part of the trip. I usually travel south on I-95 to Fort Pierce and then take the short connection there to the Florida Turnpike. It seems to help us avoid the heavy traffic in Orlando.'

'Sounds good to me. How far is it to the turnpike?' Michael asked.

'Not far. We always stop for a restroom break and a snack in Fort Pierce. Is that ok with you? It's sort of tradition.'

'Sure. I'm okay with whatever you want.'

I had to check my mile markers to make sure I didn't miss the exit. I didn't drive this way often, so it wasn't familiar to me. There! I saw my exit. 'This is Fort Pierce,' I said.

We took the exit, headed west, and found a restaurant. We stopped and stretched. 'Feels good to get out of the van,' I said.

'Sure does. How're you doing? Want me to drive?' Michael asked.

'I think I'm okay. To be honest, I'm not a great passenger. Tommy found that out a long time ago.'

'Speaking of Tommy, you haven't mentioned him much along the way. By the way, how *did* you get his van?'

'Well, you and I were talking. He didn't seem to have too much to say. That's unusual for him, I know.'

'Do you still see him?'

'No. He must have gone to the men's room.' I looked around and then shouted, 'There he is. Hey, Tom, we're over here,' I said, waving him over.

Michael sat quietly. He watched as I looked over his shoulder to see Tommy coming our way. 'Are you ready to get going?' I asked Tommy.

'Yeah, if you guys are,' he replied.

I looked at Michael and nodded. He nodded back, got up, and we went back to the van. 'I better get gas soon,' I said.

'I agree, it's a long drive on the turnpike,' Tommy said.

'I guess it's better before we get on the turnpike,' Michael agreed.

'You guys sound like a broken record,' I said. 'I'll get gas, I will.'

After gassing up, I pulled into the lane to the turnpike, grabbed a pay ticket, and drove down the long lane to the lanes on the turnpike. There wasn't much traffic today, thank goodness.

'It's about two-and-a-half hours on this part of the trip,' I remarked.

'It's a lot further than I thought,' Michael commented.

'It goes fast when we're talking and laughing. Also, I can show you the beautiful coconut palm trees. Mom says they only grow in south Florida and she loves them because they're so pretty. This is the only time I go through Miami, so it's the only time I get to see them,' I said.

We drove the many miles down the turnpike and, as promised, I showed Michael the coconut palms. He agreed they are beautiful. There really isn't anything else interesting on this part of the trip.

We finally arrived at the south end of Miami, exited the turnpike, and continued south on US Highway 1. I was told US 1 - as they call it - spans the eastern coast of the country from the southernmost point in Key West – where *mile marker O Key West* is – and goes two thousand three hundred and seventy miles north to Fort Kent, Maine at the Canadian border. I have never been that far north, but I have been to the southernmost point in Key West. I was excited to be heading there again. Tommy always said, *'It's like going home.'*

'I know it's a ways, but we have to go through the Everglades and several Keys to get to our hotel on Marathon Key,' I said.

'Ev-er-glades,' Michael said slowly.

'Yeah. I understand they are seven thousand eight hundred square miles of wetlands. They're filled with gators and snakes people didn't want anymore. They just turned the snakes loose there. I would *never* want to go there,' I said emphatically.

'Me neither. You're just a wealth of information, aren't you? What's your favorite part of visiting the Keys?' Tommy asked.

'Everything,' I said.

'Tell me more,' he continued.

'Well, Tommy always makes a plan. I did the plan this time, just the way he always did in the past.'

'What's on the list?' Michael asked.

'I like this hotel. Tommy and I stayed at the campgrounds the last few times we came, but I sprung for a hotel this time. We'll be more comfortable there. Tommy treated me for everything every time we came because I had no money when I first came to Florida. A motel was out of the budget then. After we get settled, Tommy always likes to check out the spot where he catches barracuda. Sometimes we swim there too.'

'Sounds interesting. I don't think I want to swim though.'

'It's part of the experience,' I insisted. 'Anyway, we usually get settled at the campground and it's a short day because of traveling. Then, tomorrow, we'll head to Key West and stop at No Name Key and check out the little Key Deer. They are the cutest and you will love them. Close to there is a little area with brackish water and the only gators in the keys. As I said, the majority of gators are in the Everglades, but we go way south of there, thankfully.'

'Thankfully is right!' Michael exclaimed.

'Another thing is the iguanas that roam all over the place. I guess people let them go as well the snakes in the Everglades and now they're everywhere. Look!' I pointed, 'There are several now.'

Michael turned quickly as I snapped. On the sidewalk near the trees, we spotted the green lizards doing their bouncy walk.

'I heard they're not friendly, so I always keep my distance,' I said.

'I'll do the same,' Michael said smiling. 'So, I was telling you about how difficult it was after I lost my brother, Murphy. Things just didn't seem the same and I still wanted them to be. Did you ever feel like that after losing someone?'

'Not that I can remember,' I started to say. 'Losing people we love is very tough for me too. I used to hear others talk about losing people, but I don't think I was very sympathetic because it never happened to me.'

'You never lost anyone?'

'Yes. I lost my grandpa. I loved him more than anything. It was at a very stressful time in my life and he was living with my family in West Virginia for several years before he passed. That made it a little less real for me I think; softened the *blow* so-to-speak. We lived together for many years, but not at the end.'

'That does make a difference. Murphy and I were close. Sometimes I'd think he was going to call or I would see him when I went to his house to take care of things.'

'That had to be difficult for you. You always seem to be the one doing the *dirty work*, if you know what I mean.'

'I know what you mean. My sisters and other brother are busy with other things. I don't mind, though. I loved Murphy. It's part of the loss.'

'I am so thirsty. Do you mind getting a soda from the cooler?' I changed the subject.

When we arrived at the hotel, I was relieved. It is a very long drive. We checked in and took our things to our room. 'I want to check the television guide quickly before we head to the fishing site if that's ok with you,' I said nonchalantly.

'Ok with me,' Michael said.

I picked up the guide and said, 'Hey, the *Blues Brothers* is on tonight. Did I ever tell you about that movie?'

'No. You never did.' Michael said as he started to unpack.

'Well, the last time Tommy and I came to the Keys, we were at the campground and I was up early as usual waiting for him. When he finally woke and stepped out of the van, he said, '*Let me put my contacts in and we'll go to Key West for Key Lime pie. It's 160 miles to Chicago, we have a half tank of gas and a half a pack of cigarettes, it's dark and we're wearing sunglasses...*' I wasn't really paying attention to him and missed what he was trying to say. I turned to him and cluelessly said slowly like I was thinking about what he said, '*You're crazy, it's like ... 1500 miles to Chicago...*' Then he said, '*No, it's the Blue's Brothers. That's my kind of humor. Some people don't like it, but I do.*' I got it then and said, '*Oh, the Blues Brothers. I remember them.*' We went for pie.'

Michael listened intently. That's what I liked best about him. I could tell him anything. I could never remember if I'd already told him a story, but he never said.

'Sounds like you had a great time,' he said.

'We always did. He made my life better. He always said that and, at first, I didn't realize it, but I do now. He taught me how to live and love life and everything in it. I spent too much time working and never had the money to do much. He always pays and takes me to the nicest places. It has been the biggest blessing of my life. I always have fun and the best part is being with him. Can we watch *The Blue's Brothers* tonight?'

'Sure.' He smiled.

We settled in and then went back to the van. Tommy had his fishing pole and tackle box. Tommy's fishing spot is close to the hotel, so we were there in no time. As we neared the spot, I did the usual U-turn on the road and drove down the small slope to park near the water.

Tommy fished as I showed Michael the rocks near the water. As we looked into the shallow ocean water, a large manta ray – or possibly stingray – swam near the rocks, 'Look!' I said loudly and pointed. I grabbed my camera and stepped onto the rocks and, as I lifted my hands to take the picture, he quickly swam away. 'Darn, I wanted that picture. I didn't realize he can see me.'

'Looks like they see everything,' Michael

laughed.

We walked along the rocks a little longer but when we came back, I didn't see Tommy. 'Where did he go?' I asked.

'Maybe he went back without us.'

'How could he do that, we have the van,' I said somewhat defiantly.

'We'll see when we get back.'

'Alright. Let's get some things for supper and snacks.'

'Now you're talking my talk,' Michael said with a smile as he rubbed his hands together.

We drove to the store, picked what we wanted, paid, and went back to the hotel. 'Tom!' I called when we got to the room. There was no answer. 'He's not here either.'

'Give it some time. Let's get supper started.'

We opened our potato salad and made sandwiches with turkey lunchmeat. I made Tommy one with lots of mayonnaise. That's the way he likes his. There were two beds, so Michael snuggled up on one and I took the other.

'The movie's on!' I said excitedly.

'Great,' Michael said.

We had to watch that two-and-a-half-hour movie for two hours before Dan Akroyd said that line Tommy liked so well. I stayed awake, but Michael dozed long before that part came on.

I let him sleep and fell asleep myself after the movie. Tommy's sandwich remained on the plate 'til morning.

9

Our First Day in the Keys

It was our first full day in the Keys! YEAH! I was excited to show Michael everything. We had a quick breakfast of cold cereal at the hotel. The sandwich I made for Tommy the evening before was still on the table where I left it. Michael discarded it before I noticed it. How thoughtful of him.

As we drove from Marathon Key across the seven-mile bridge – a modern marvel that is part of the Overseas Highway that connects Knights Key to Little Duck Key - I told Michael how, each time we drove across this long bridge, Tommy told me the story of the day he jogged across it while his mother and sister waited for him on the other side. He said it took him over an hour. I always thought it was extremely patient of his family to wait for him. I also thought about how wonderfully healthy he was then compared to now. I always say time marches mercilessly on and on and takes its toll on each of us as well as each person I love.

I am awed at how the water is everywhere you looked – the Atlantic Ocean was to our left and the Gulf of Mexico to our right as we drove along what seemed to be just a strip of road running between waterways. And, while driving on the seven-mile bridge, there was just the ocean waters flowing under us.

Next, we passed through Bahia Honda Key. 'We have to walk up there later,' I said excitedly as I pointed to a bridge extending from the Key high over the ocean. 'Tommy and I always take a walk up where the unfinished bridge is. Or maybe it was damaged by a storm. I can never remember. I don't worry about remembering because Tommy tells me the story every time we come.'

Michael didn't seem to mind my rambling. He just smiled and nodded occasionally as we drove along.

When we came to No Name Key, I made a right-hand turn and then slowed the car as we combed the neighborhood like villains. It's easy to think this, but the folks who live here are accustomed to tourists like us driving around slowly, looking towards their yards and homes in search of the cutest little dear I've ever seen.

'There!' I shouted as I pointed at three little deer grazing in someone's front yard. I was just a wealth of information and added, 'When the deer see people, they think they're going to be fed, so they come right up to you. You'll love this. I brought some apple slices for them. Here...' I handed Michael the fruit slices.

Michael was surprisingly happy to take the apple slices. He had to bend *way* over to offer the snacks to the little deer because he was over six feet tall. One of the deer had a large antler rack. All of them were so small, each about the size of a large dog. This makes them cute to see because they look like large deer, only tiny. Safer too. Full-sized deer can be dangerous because they are so big, strong, and unpredictable.

We stayed a while and pet them as we fed them. The deer seemed to like all the attention. In the distance, we could see a family putting out treats for deer that visited their home. *'How fun it must be to have a home here,'* I thought.

Seemingly able to read my mind, Michael said, 'Wouldn't it be cool to live here?'

'That's just what I was thinking,' I replied. 'We could see these little ones every day and give them treats!' Michael smiled as I tightened my body like an excited child does when they're happy.

When we ran out of apple slices, we headed back to the car, promising the deer we'd be back with more treats tomorrow.

'Do you think they understand?' Michael said and chuckled softly.

'Yes, I do,' I said. 'They'll be waiting, I'm sure.' Michael didn't dispute this.

We continued our drive to Key West. When we passed the army base Tommy was stationed at years ago, I looked in the back seat expecting to see Tommy, but he wasn't there. I was puzzled and tried to remember why he didn't come with us. I turned to Michael and said, 'I was just going to ask Tommy to tell us the story about the eel and his friends, Rex and Sumara, but he's not with us. Did he stay back at the hotel?'

'He didn't say anything to me,' Michael said as he looked out his window.

'Huh,' I mused. 'Well, it looks like it's just you and me.'

'I'm ok with that.'

'Well, I can tell you all about how Tommy and his friends snorkeled in these ocean waters and caught and ate lobster and barracuda and all kinds of things.' I twisted my face at the odd things Tommy liked to eat besides the lobster and then continued, 'Tommy said his friends taught him everything about the ocean because they came from Hawaii and seemingly knew everything.'

'That's interesting,' Michael said. 'How did they catch the lobster?'

'I'm not sure. I think they used a net or something.'

'Must have enjoyed them.'

I thought for a moment and said, 'They did according to Tommy and that's not all they caught... but oh! Tommy said once he was in the water and something *huge* swam right by him.' I moved my hands in a large circle in the air to indicate something huge and looked at Michael and continued,' I think I would have *freaked* by that time! I'm a big chicken.'

Michael was quiet, but appeared to be captivated and interested. I asked, 'Are you wishing I didn't have more stories?'

'No, I like your stories,' Michael said looking my way with a reassuring smile.

I didn't know how Michael and I had become such good friends, but I was really liking it about now. We drove the few more miles to Key West and I continued to dazzle him with all the tales Tommy told me.

When we arrived in Key West, I asked, 'How about if we ride around the island? Is that ok? It's pretty small and doesn't take too long.'

'Sure,' Michael was so agreeable. 'I'd like to see it.'

We turned and started to make our way around the island. As we passed the White Street Pier, I touted another Tommy story. I turned again to look for Tommy in the back seat for affirmation that I had the story correct, but he still wasn't there. This confused me. I remembered asking Michael about him earlier and we decided that for some reason, Tommy stayed at the hotel.

But Tommy never stayed behind. He was usually the leader of the group and showing us all the sites and taking us to each one every time we visited the Keys. He rattled on and on about every attraction and every experience he had here. This trip seemed so different. All of a sudden, I felt like I was the 'cruise director.'

As all these thoughts went round and round in my mind, I seemed to drive aimlessly around the island. I saw all the people having fun and talking and sharing a meal or shopping. Some were bicycle riding, some were visiting the local fishing boats, and some were just enjoying the sun and ocean life here.

'Something wrong?' Michael asked in a truly concerned tone.

'Nothing's wrong,' I said slowly. 'I'm just a little confused… Not sure…' I stammered.

'Is there something I can do to help?'

'I'm not sure. I just want to show you the island.'

'Let's do it,' Michael replied and slapped his knee. 'Do you mind stopping for a soda? I only brought one with us. I underestimated the heat here.'

'Sure. There's a small store just ahead.'

I turned into the store parking lot and Michael went in to buy a soda. I was outside the car when Tommy came my way. 'Where're you been?' I asked, happy to see him.

'I'm here.'

'I've been telling Michael about all our past adventures here. He's having a great time. Want to share more of your stories?'

Tommy said, 'I think you're doing just fine.' He climbed in the back seat as Michael came back to the car, soda in hand.

'What do you want to do next?' he asked.

'Well, there's an aquarium we can visit. Let me find a parking spot at the State Park.'

'Sounds good. What's your favorite part of Key West?' Michael seemed to know instinctively that I needed a distraction.

'I love it all but I love the butterfly house / museum at the end of Duval Street,' I started to say, 'But, I also enjoy the State Park and there's a small beach area where we can swim in the ocean.'

'Sure. Whatever you want to do is fine with me. The aquarium sounds good too.'

After some thought, I said, 'You know, I haven't been to many places. I hear the mountains in Colorado are great and so are our National Forests. And, of course, there's the Grand Canyon. I hear it's spectacular....' I rambled.

'I've traveled some, not much myself. Why do you bring that up?'

'Well, I guess Key West may seem boring to some... and I hope you're not bored...'

'No, not at all. This is very interesting to me,' he interrupted. 'I enjoy the islands and the water and being with you is pretty nice too!' He smiled.

'We can't forget how fun I am to be with,' I said a little sarcastically.

'You are. And I like those cute little deer you introduced me to.' We both smiled.

Being grateful for the reassurance, I continued, 'Well, the Keys are so special to me because of Tommy. Now I can share them with you and that makes me happy too. I'm sorry to go on and on about all the things Tommy said and what we did here, but I spent so much of my time with him. And, even though he's sick, we still come and he always has a list of things for us to do…' I began to ponder what I really meant to say and what I was really feeling. I was getting a little mixed up.

Michael interrupted my thoughts, 'I want you to tell me everything. It's important to you and I don't mind. I like the stories. I like seeing you excited about the time you spent with him and how much it meant to you and still does.'

I could tell Michael meant it. He was so willing to let me just talk and talk. Now that I think about it, so were my friends and family. Every time I called recently, they let me talk and talk. They never seemed busy or had something they had to get to.

Somehow, I got the sense Michael and others felt sorry for me and I couldn't understand why anyone would feel sorry for me. I was having such a good time.

10

In Memorandum

Oh no, our last day! Time certainly does go by too fast. I was excited to be in the Keys again and we had such fun, but we knew this last day would come. Michael seemed to be enjoying his time here too.

The door of the hotel room opened and Michael entered with his breakfast in hand. 'I'm going to try these pancakes today,' he said with a smile.

'I'm going to get something. Will you be ready to go soon?' I asked.

'I think so,' Michael said. 'What's on the agenda today?'

'Well, I thought we'd do another bike ride. We can rent the same bikes in Key West and ride around the areas we didn't see yet. Then we can stop for Key Lime pie. Key West is famous for it and it's Tommy's favorite thing to do after a ride.'

'Sounds great,' Michael said as he put an

entire pancake in his mouth.

'That's too much pancake!' I said adamantly. I laughed and left the room.

When I returned with yogurt and a banana, Michael was ready to go.

We hopped in the car and headed south. 'Are you going to tell me about Tommy jogging across this seven-mile bridge again?' Michael asked with a sly smile on his face.

'No,' I said matter-of-factly. 'I know what you're doing. You're making fun of my repeating my stories. I'm sorry for that. That bothers most people, but Tommy did it all the time and I wish he would tell us his stories all over again.'

'No, no. I'm not poking fun. It's one of my favorite things about you. I'm just playing around.'

When we arrived in Key West, I made the turn into the rental store and we picked out two bikes. 'I still like that bicycle-built-for-two over there, but that might not be comfortable up and down the hills here,' I mentioned.

'How about we do the same bikes today and think about the one built for two tomorrow or later if we ride again?'

'We're going home tomorrow,' I said sort of sadly.

'Oh yeah. I almost forgot. Lost track of the days.'

'Me too,' I said. 'Well, we can do some fun things today. I know the way, so follow me.'

'I rode with you the other day remember? I

think I know this small island pretty well now. You're a good guide.'

I shot him a look and said, 'But you don't know what I have in mind today! Can I still be the leader?'

'Aye, aye, Captain,' Michael saluted with one eye squinted.

'Very funny,' I said. 'You don't know the island as well as you think you do, I do.'

'Well, that's certainly true,' Michael laughed. 'Lead on.'

We rode out of the parking lot and headed west to make an entire circle around the island.

'I want to show you the 'Southern Most Point' monument,' I said.

'Sounds good.'

Michael was always so agreeable. When we arrived at the monument, the area was packed with tourists; too many to get close enough for a picture so we decided to come back. As its name implies, it is the southern-most point in America and is an iconic landmark. It lets us know there are ninety miles to Cuba! Ha ha.

We headed around Mallory Square and some small shops near the square. Then we rode toward Duval Street when I spotted the cemetery Tommy and I visited once.

I made a quick left turn into the cemetery. 'Hey, where're we going?' Michael snapped. He almost fell trying to keep up with my turn.

'I want to show something funny,' I shouted

back at him.

Michael followed as we made our way to the back section of the cemetery. Finally, I spotted what I wanted to show him but, all of a sudden, a strange feeling came over me. I was filled with sadness. I stopped by the gravestone and had a flashback of taking Tommy's picture as he posed and pointed to the epitaph that says, 'I told you I was sick.'

'You wanted to show me this?' Michael asked, slightly out of breath.

'Well, I wanted you to see how we thought this was so funny when we found it. Tommy heard about it because it was on the evening news once and he always wanted to find it when we came to the Keys. When we did, he stood by the stone and I took his picture. I remember it like it was yesterday.'

I paused for a moment and it seemed Michael could see the wheels turning in my mind. 'Tell me more,' he finally said.

'We laughed because no one seems to realize how ill Tommy is and he tells me he feels like he may pass soon, but I try to encourage him that we don't know when that may happen.'

I paused again and then continued, 'Once, when we were driving home from a movie, Tommy said I didn't know how sick he is and I told him that's the reason I'm here. Here in Florida with him, I meant,' I motioned 'here' to Michael as he nodded.

'Tommy was silent and I never admitted to knowing how ill he is. I don't want him to feel worse than he already does. I know how scared he is. He just doesn't talk about it much. I feel so helpless and wonder how life will be without him.' My whole life has revolved around him for over three years. Not to mention how close we have been all our lives.

'I can just imagine how difficult all this has been for you,' Michael said softly.

Then, we both looked up to see a funeral procession arriving. Suddenly, I was frozen. A wave of sorrow came over me. I wanted to cry but couldn't seem to. I wanted to speak but the words didn't want to come out.

'Do you want to go?' Michael asked. He tried to help me back on my bicycle so we could leave.

'I don't know. I feel anxious now. I don't know why. I'm not sure what's wrong with me. My stomach feels like I'm going to get sick.'

Then, I felt like I was in a dream. I felt like everything around me was moving in slow motion and I couldn't make myself move along faster. I was queasy inside and felt afraid. I once heard grief was like fear, but why was I feeling this way? I remembered a black car and all our friends and family.

Memories were flashing in my mind about finding Tommy slumped in a chair. I shook all these images off and shouted, 'We need to go back to the hotel now please!'

'Okay, okay. Let's ride the bikes back to the

rental store and we can go back.'

'Why didn't Tommy come with us today? Was he sleeping when we left?' I began asking these and many more questions.

Michael stayed very calm and spoke softly and slowly to me, 'He's probably watching television or something at the hotel. Let's go see.'

I peddled as quickly as I was able. Michael did all he could to keep up with me.

Finally, we arrived back at the store, returned the bicycles, hopped in the car, and I drove faster than usual back to the hotel.

'I enjoyed the ride,' Michael tried to help break my anxiety.

'So did I.'

'What do you want to do next?'

'I want to see Tommy,' I stated.

'What happened back at the cemetery?'

'I don't know,' I started. 'I got all these weird feelings. I'm so confused. I don't know what I think and what I'm feeling or why I'm feeling this way.' I just blabbered.

It seemed like a hundred years, but we finally arrived back at the hotel. I raced to the room and, after I opened the door, I called, 'Tommy! Tommy, are you here?'

There was no answer. I looked through the suitcases but didn't see anything that was Tommy's. I opened his travel bag and saw his wetsuit, mask, snorkel, and fins. 'Here are some of his things.'

'Yes. I see,' Michael said slowly. He watched me frantically look for Tommy and more of Tommy's things.

'He isn't here,' I said and started to cry.

Michael put his arms around me. 'I'm here. We'll figure this out together.'

'Figure what out? Where is he?'

'Not sure. Let's think about it.'

'Well, he came with us. Now I don't see him. His breakfast is still here.'

I saw the blueberry yogurt and banana I left for Tommy sitting on the table in the corner of the room.

'Are you sure he's still here?' I asked Michael.

'What are you thinking?'

'I don't know. I've been so caught up in showing you the Keys, I forgot about Tommy. Why didn't he come with us to Key West and bike ride with us? It's his favorite thing to do. And he loves those little Key deer and Key Lime pie as much as I do.'

I just kept rambling and, when I felt completely exhausted, I asked Michael, 'Do you mind if I rest for a while?'

'No. Not at all.' He has an unusual look on his face – it was a mixture of sadness and concern. I was too tired to try to understand or even ask what he was thinking.

I curled up on the bed and fell asleep.

When I woke, Michael was lounging on his

bed, reading.

'Feel better?' he asked.

'Yes, but I'm still confused.'

'I'm sure you are.'

'I see Tommy's things but still don't see him with us. How did this happen?'

'I don't know. Seems he isn't here,' Michael said softly.

'Well, what do you want to do for supper?'

'Whatever you want is fine with me,' Michael replied, surprised how I changed the subject so quickly.

'There's a great seafood restaurant close by. How about that? We could do burgers or steak too if you want.'

'Seafood sounds fab! Let's do it,' he said with a smile.

I stopped, looked at him, and asked, 'Do you think I'm crazy?'

'No,' is all he said.

We had our meal and then sat on rocks on the Gulf side of the ocean to watch the sun go down on another perfect, lovely day in the Florida Keys.

It reminded me of the times my mother and sisters and I ran to the east side of the St. Joseph peninsula every morning to watch the sun come up when we vacationed there. Then, after we enjoyed our day at the beach and meals and sometimes shopped or had ice cream, we always ran like children again to the west side of the peninsula to watch the sun set to conclude another day.

My memories seemed to be playing tricks on me. They flooded my mind all at once and I couldn't keep them all organized. Tommy's face kept coming to my mind and the things he said and the ways he looked at me when we were together. What was happening to me?

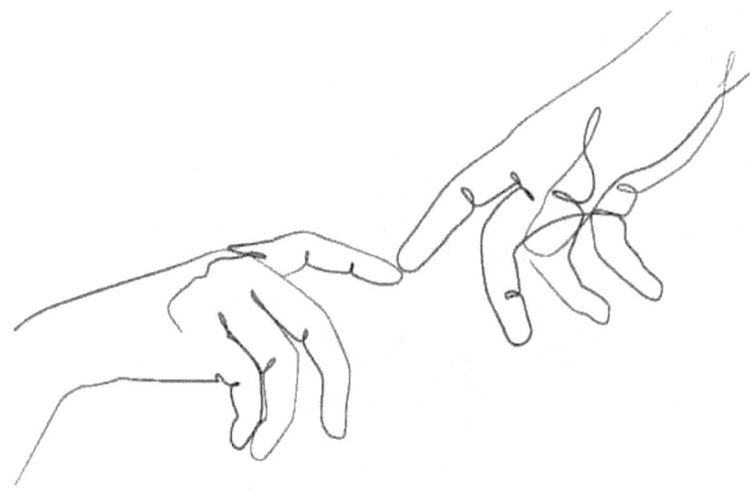

11

Heading Home

As we headed home, we were both unnaturally silent. I never seemed to shut up and Michael was usually pleasantly chatty. I glanced over to see him staring out the window as we traveled the seven hours out of the Keys, northbound on the Florida turnpike to home.

'What do you have planned when we get home?' Michael asked, breaking the silence.

'I have to find Tommy. I think I don't understand what happened to him.'

'I can stay with you for a few days.'

'That's ok. I'm fine.' I lied. I was torn inside with mixed feelings of confusion and sadness and loneliness and loss for some reason I couldn't quite put my finger on.

'I want to,' he insisted.

'Ok. It may be nice to have some company.'

The seven hours passed and we pulled into my driveway. 'I want to check the house and then I'll gather my things from the car.'

Michael smiled, 'I'll start unloading my things.'

I ran to open the door and looked everywhere for signs of Tommy, but there weren't any. I found a picture of the two of us on a table in my hallway and stared at it for several minutes.

'Are you ok?' Michael asked.

'I'm not sure.'

'Can I help?'

'Can you come with me after I get my things from the car?'

'Sure,' he said.

We organized everything we brought home and Michael made us each a sandwich, 'Here. You haven't eaten anything since breakfast,' he said as he handed me a double-decker club sandwich made with vegetables we left a week ago.

'Let's go,' I snapped.

It was a challenge to get back into that car after that long trip home, but we did it. The first stop was the apartment complex Tommy stayed in. 'I thought he lived with you?' Michael asked as if making a statement.

'Well, he does, but he has this apartment too.'

Tommy's van wasn't in his handicapped parking place. *That's odd. I wonder where his van is?* I mused. I knew I wasn't making any sense, but Michael didn't push the conversation. We climbed the stairs to apartment E. 'I'll knock.'

Michael nodded as I tapped on the door. No

answer. A couple walked up the stairs and the woman asked, 'Can we help you?'

'I'm looking for Tommy,' I said.

'There's no Tommy here.'

I was puzzled, but Michael swooped in to rescue me and said, 'Thank you very much, we'll try another apartment.' He ushered me down the stairs and back to our car.

'What's wrong?' I asked.

'Nothing's *wrong*,' he started to say. 'How are you?'

'I'm fine. Just confused.'

'I realize that. I think we need to talk.'

'About what?'

'You and Tommy.'

'What about me and Tommy? Oh,' I said with that *the light-just-turned-on-in-my-head* look, 'I'm going to go to the store around the corner. Sometimes he goes there. He takes walks and shops for groceries.'

'Ok. Let's go.'

As we arrived at the grocery store, I looked around but didn't see his van. 'That's strange,' I said. 'I don't think he's here either.'

'What happened in Key West when we saw the funeral?' Michael was unusually firm and direct.

'I'm not sure. I had a picture of Tommy in my mind that he was slumped over in a chair.'

'Tell me more,' Michael rolled his hand, motioning for me to continue.

'I have this picture in my mind of all our friends and families together - like they were at the cemetery - and I don't know why. It seems I had this dream and I can't make sense of it all.'

'Tell me more.'

'Well…. what makes you think there's more? I don't understand the bad feelings inside of me. I want to run away from them and feel like if I can find Tommy, they'll go away.'

'What feelings?'

'I feel sad and tired and anxious and scared all at the same time. I feel like I just can't make sense of things and want to cry but I can't seem to. I keep picturing Tommy and me doing the things we always did – I mean kayaking on the water, eating pizza together, watching movies on his television. I can even see him lying on the floor next to me as he rests because he had such a difficult time breathing sometimes….' I started to hesitate.

'Go on.'

I repeated myself, 'Then, that funeral made me think of Tommy for some reason. I remember all these people came to visit but Tommy wasn't there. They all talked about him and there was a huge black car…'

'Like the one at the cemetery?'

'Yes. Exactly like that…..'

As I sat pondering, some things began to be very clear. 'Where is Tommy now?' Michael asked.

'I don't know. I can't find him. But we talked just the other day. I told you about it.'

'Yes. I remember,' Michael said patiently.

Then, I began to cry. 'Did something happen to Tommy?'

'You tell me.'

Things began to become clearer to me. The memories were unclear, then clear, and then I said, 'I came to his apartment and I found him in his chair. He made a sandwich and he was just about to eat it…' I cried harder.

'Take your time,' Michael said as he put his arm around my shoulder.

'I called his name, but he didn't answer. He didn't smile back at me. He was still and he was cold. I think…… I think Tommy died. Oh, no.'

Michael didn't answer me. I saw tears in his eyes too.

I fell into Michael's arms and bawled and bawled. In fact, I wailed. It seemed like I cried forever. Two hours later, I was still crying. He never rushed me. 'What am I going to do?' I asked without expecting an answer. 'What am I going to do?'

'We'll figure it all out,' Michael said in broken words fighting back more tears.

'But I have been going places with him and talking to him,' I started to say, suddenly realizing how crazy that sounded.

'We know. You have had some confusing moments.'

'Tell me. Is he really gone?'

'I think so.'

'Am I crazy? Am I imagining him?'

'No. You're not crazy. You just miss him.'

'How long ago did he leave us?' I turned my tear-stained face toward Michael and begged for the answers I couldn't arrive at myself.

'Oh, I think it's been about a year now.'

'A whole year?!!!??' I was shocked. 'No way.'

'Well, I have to check. I'm not exactly sure.'

'You knew? Did everyone know? Do they think I'm losing it? Lost it really.' I rambled.

'We knew but we could see how hurt you've been.' Michael was so gentle with me.

'Is everyone worried about me?'

'We've all been close for some time now.'

'What am I going to do?' I asked again.

'We're here for you. We'll help you get through this.'

We were quiet for a while and the tears came again and then I was quiet again and then the tears came again. I fell asleep.

When I woke up, Michael and some other friends and family were around me. Michael had a letter from Tommy. It said, *'I want to thank you for all the friendship we've shared over the years and for loving me so. I want to thank you for going everywhere with me and doing all the things I loved – the Keys, the rivers, the movies, lunch, the bike rides, the pizza, home movies, and more. I also love you for shopping for me, doing my wash, cooking, and taking those miserably difficult-to-remove covers off the tops of my lemonade and orange juice bottles. (haha) If you're reading this note, I have gone off to heaven, but will never leave you completely. I will always watch over you and want you to remember me fondly - the way I will always remember you. Love, Tommy.'*

Now what was I going to do? I felt like my whole world was crashing in on me -again. Somewhere in my mind, I remembered being sad about Tommy leaving this world and me and I was overwhelmed again, just like then.

'We're here. You're not alone,' my dear Aunt said to me. I had the faintest memory of her talking to me as I drove out of the Keys several years ago. That must have been when I lost Tommy and didn't know how to cope with it all. I was depressed and confused and so many other conflicting feelings overwhelmed me.

I was trying to stop all the bad feelings when I realized how sorry I was for Tommy to have been so sick. I was sorry that he was alone when he went to heaven. I was sorry I didn't do more. I was sorry he had to go through all these things. I was sorry he was scared. I was sorry he went to the doctors and they told him bad news. I could only imagine how he felt as we did all the fun things we did and he never knew if it would be the last time he did these things. I couldn't bear all the feelings so I ditched them.

'You have to face these feelings now so they don't hurt you anymore,' I heard Michael say in his kindest voice.

'I don't think I can, it hurts too much,' I said.

'It won't hurt like this forever, just for a while if you work through it all. It's called grief.' I knew my Aunt knew all about this because she lost so many people she loved and knew exactly how I felt. She just wanted me to be ok.

98

12

Good Grief

To be honest, I know very little about grief. The only thing I *was* sure of is that I didn't like it very much.

The next few months were torture. Everywhere I looked, I wanted to see Tommy, but he was nowhere to be found.

It was so odd to me because I was so sure he was with me recently as we floated down the river and drove to different stores. He was with me for Jeopardy and pizza days too. I was sure of it, or so I thought.

I still wanted to talk to him, so sometimes I did even when I couldn't see his face. I just didn't tell anyone. I'd take a picture of him and tell him all about my day and how much I missed him.

The sadness was overwhelming at times. It seemed to come over me suddenly like a dark cloud in the sky. Then, I would feel better. My aunt said this is grief and gets better but I am skeptical. There seems no end in sight to the feelings churning in the pit of my stomach, the tears that flow without any provocation, and all the memories that keep flooding my mind.

I wanted to talk about Tommy, but couldn't find anyone with time to talk about him, so I just made up my mind to do it alone. I was afraid they would think I was still crazy.

One day I made Tommy a sandwich before I remembered he wasn't really with me. When Michael caught me doing this, he let me off the hook by saying, 'Wasn't it so nice of you to make me a sandwich!'

We both smiled. He was my constant companion and I was grateful. I'm not sure what I would have done without him. He knew when to talk, when to sit quietly, when I needed a hug, when I needed to sleep, and when I needed to share the same memories over and over.

My hygiene suffered a little. Some say grief is responsible. That grief thing sure gets a bad rap – and I think it's well-deserved to be honest. When Michael suggested I wash up, I always said, 'Maybe tomorrow.'

Meals were spotty too. Sometimes I was so hungry I could eat everything in the fridge, but sometimes I went days without eating.

When we were out, just the slightest thing threatened to send me reeling into a tailspin of emotions that made me feel like I was on a rollercoaster. For instance, one time my aunt and cousin and I decided to visit the home and garden show where they were singing songs in one corner of the huge warehouse hosting the event. When they sang, *The Slow Lane* by Jimmy Buffet, I burst into weepy tears. That was one of our favorite songs. Tommy played a variety of music when we went anywhere and this was one of his faves.

Michael never left my side. My family didn't talk much about my 'seeing' and 'talking' to Tommy for almost an entire year after I came to terms with his passing. 'Passing' was nicer to say than death. Dead and death are awful words. The counselor said I was just not ready to accept that he was gone. He said some people do what I did when the loss is extremely great and traumatic. It's how our minds protect us from the great sadness we feel when we lose the ones we love this much. I didn't know anyone else who did what I did but, in any event, he made me feel better.

All I know is I don't wish grief on anyone, but then I realize the only other option is to never love anyone and I don't want that option to ever be an option in my life.

When I needed, really needed, to talk to Tommy, I hid and did it where no one could see me. I think they suspected though because I heard murmurings going on when I walked into rooms where my loved ones were.

They told me everyone grieves in their own way and in their own time. *They* told me grief was a normal process in life and there were stages I was going to have to go through to get through it. I wondered what stage I was in and how long it would take before I felt normal again. They all assured me I was going to be fine.

Fine. What is fine? Living life without the one I loved so much. Living life as if it were the same and untainted by pain and loss? What would ever be *normal* again?

I had to walk this lonely path to see where it would lead and what the answers were to all these questions. No one could walk through the fire of grief but me. It was my grief and mine alone. They missed Tommy too. This I knew, but I didn't know their grief and no one lived mine. I know my God knew my grief and He would always help me through. He did.

It was true - I was still here. The store where I shopped for Tommy was still here. The apartment he lived in was still here. The rivers that flowed from headsprings with millions of gallons of water pouring into the runs each day were still here. The restaurants we went to were still here. But Tommy wasn't here. I just couldn't wrap my head around it.

I made plans to kayak our favorite river. When I went down the run, I spotted some manatees. 'Hello, gorgeous,' I called. 'I was told you don't come up this river and here you are.' I felt it was as if Tommy was telling me everything was going to be alright.

Michael came over most nights. We watched

television and had dinners. We talked about everything. Day after day passed and I still think about Tommy every day, but the pain has lessened. The tears have stopped flowing. I have a small memorial with Tommy's pictures and his photo albums. I will never forget even though, thankfully, the pain has lessened.

Michael and I laugh about it being like pulling teeth for him, my family, and other friends to bring me back to the land of the living, but they all managed to save me somehow. I am truly grateful. Love is great. Life is great. I know Tommy would want me to 'carry on.' I am.

13

Thank You Tommy

As I sit and look at all the pictures Tommy and I took together – and we took a lot, I say, 'Thank you, Tommy.'

'Thank you, Tommy, for being in my life, being my friend, loving me, and letting me love you. You have made my life extraordinary. I wasn't even aware how much I needed what you freely gave me.'

'Thank you, Tommy, for taking me to so many places and giving me so many new memories when I thought there were no more memories for me to create.'

'Thank you, Tommy, for treating me like I was 'Queen for a Day!' each and every day we spent together. You treated me to fancy lunches and movies when funds were so low, I couldn't treat myself.'

'Thank you, Tommy, for teaching me to work hard but to play hard as well and enjoy every moment of every day because tomorrow may not come. I know you lived this way until tomorrow did not come for you.'

'Thank you, Tommy, for taking me places like the springs and the Keys and Kelly's Island and Put-in-Bay, and camping, and fishing, and more to experience fun things I would never have done without you. You protected me everywhere we went and made sure I had everything I needed.'

'Thank you, Tommy, for letting me care for you when you needed it. It was my pleasure to wash your clothes and grocery shop. I knew we were in trouble when you allowed me to push you in a wheelchair to Rick's room because you couldn't make it on your own.'

'Thank you, Tommy, for showing me how to be brave in life and in death. I am so sorry you felt frightened and I'm so sorry I couldn't change the things we never wanted to happen. I don't like feeling helpless, but know we come into this world with no effort of our own and we leave it just the same. Control is an illusion. No one but the God we love is in control.'

'Thank you, Tommy, for making me love fudge. I know how much you enjoyed it and I do too now. I also enjoy the peanut butter and jelly sandwiches we shared. I will never forget sitting at that picnic table so many years ago when we were the only ones in the park after kayaking. You may not have much in this world, but you gave me all you had. You gave me *you*. You gave me time. You gave me things money cannot buy and cannot be achieved without the love of a friend. I now know the most precious thing I could have given you or any friend was just *me*, my time, my love. I will try to do this every, every day, my dear friend.'

As I sat, I began to cry. I wanted to say more and more. How could this be all I had to say to him? How could I tell him how much everything meant to me and how much I will miss him and want to be where we were together so I could still feel close to him even though he wasn't with me any longer? I wanted to say thank you for every little thing and every big thing. I never wanted the moments with him to end and I didn't want this special time of remembering to end either. I just didn't *want* to let go.

I drifted to sleep and had the most wonderful dream. I dreamt Tommy was well. He could breathe and he could run over the seven-mile bridge again. I dreamt he was scuba diving with Frank and catching lobster. Tommy wasn't afraid, he was happy, so happy. He was happier than I ever saw him. I hear in his voice. I was happy too. It was so nice to see him and be with him and, when rode the bikes, he never had to stop to catch his breath and, when he walked with me, he talked the whole time. He was never able to do this before.

I asked him, 'Do you know I love you?'

Then, Tommy looked into my eyes and said, 'I know. I love you too. I always will. I will always be with you. I will always want the best for you. I want you to be happy and come and see me again soon.'

There was such a precious peace about my sleep this day. I was having *'sweet dreams'* and *sweet* they were. When I woke, I realized I was dreaming. But then I realized I believe it was me seeing Tommy in heaven where he was well and able to do all the things he was no longer able to do here. How could I not be happy for him? I was unhappy for me. I missed him. I was torn. I cried again.

I sat and cried for several hours and then I closed our photo albums and placed them with the other memorabilia that I have collected over the years to remind me of Tommy.

I made a decision that day to be a better person and try to make everyone's life better that I possibly could. I decided it was time for me to tell the people in my life how much I appreciated them and how much they did to help me be the person I am today. I was foolish to think they just *knew*. How could they know? I never told them. Things are going to be different. I am going to be different. Tommy changed me forever. Love changed me for the better.

'Thank you, Tommy. Thank you with all my heart. I can't wait to see you again. I know I will one day. I will be home soon, but not too soon. Wait for me!'

14

Looking Back
How It All Worked Out

Well, I'm back. Today I feel as if I've returned from being gone on a long journey - gone a long way away - mentally that is. Back to reality, they tell me. I'm packing to drive to the Keys. Tommy's right, it *is* like going home. I have plans. I made a list. Gonna see me some little deer, take me a bike ride around Key West, stop to have a piece of key lime pie, order a second piece for my friend (who is in my heart), and think of that friend. And more.

I promised myself 'no tears' this time. I am committed to making every memory happy. Tommy once said, 'Even the good memories are sad.' I know what he meant because he lost so much along his way and his good memories were inseparable from the tough ones. But I was determined for my memories to make me happy. I may even stop at the cemetery to see the sign on the famous person's grave Tommy and I visited the last time we were in Key West together that said *I Told You I Was Sick* and laugh as I remember taking the photo of Tommy pointing to it.

I realize now that he's not here *in person* any longer, but Michael was right, I don't have to let him go and stop pretending he's with me. In fact, Michael told me to just not tell anyone. This will be my plan. Plus, I think the ones we love that pass on to heaven are watching over us - like our own little cheering squad of guardian angels. I don't say this out loud though because I don't want anyone reporting me to the 'men in the white coats!'

I think about things - maybe more than most. I know life is short and I need to live the life I've been given. Others still need me here. In my mind, I know I need to think about the ones I lost to make myself happy I had them but I need to carry on. Dad always said, *'Don't be sad it's over, be glad it happened.'*

Boy, am I glad it happened. I'm glad I came to Florida to spend time with my family. Glad for the way Tommy and others made my life better and made me a better person. However, I always wanted my happy times to go on forever. I guess everyone does. I always said, *'The beginning of something always seems happier than the end of something.'* But, when one thing ends, another can begin, I guess. This is the cycle of this life as we know it and, sometimes, we need to decide to continue being unhappy about the loss or look forward to the next chapter.

Sometimes extreme happiness floods my very being and sometimes I feel crushed by overwhelming waves of sadness and loss. It's a mixed-up time, but the sadness is less and less and the happiness is more and more.

Looking back on it all, yeah, I guess I did go a little crazy. Just couldn't let go of Tommy. He was one of the few people who made my life better. He was my whole life focus for three and a half years and then, suddenly, it was over. So many memories. So many happy times and now, gone. I couldn't figure out what to do for a while because I hadn't done anything but be with Tommy for so long. Michael was the only other friend I had outside of my family.

I decided this trip to the Keys would be 'like going home,' just like Tommy always said. I will get there ... and remember. Will kiss the little Key dear, and remember. Will try to fish for Barracuda so I can remember. I'll visit the *one or two* gators in the Keys and remember. I will visit the Butterfly Museum and the Aquarium, walk down Duval Street, park in the Fort Zachary State Park parking lot, and remember. I will ride my bicycle past the Hemingway House and remember. I am so thankful for so many things to remember.

I couldn't walk into my future because I was holding on so tightly to my past, the past that I yearn for that will never be back. The talks, the walks, the lunches, the movies, the rivers, the Keys, the everything. The casual everyday things we did. I will always miss him. I need to make the new memories Tommy said we were making as we made all of ours.

So, I'm packing my mask, snorkel, and fins, my kayak, and my bike. There's a great ocean beach by the State Park for snorkeling and swimming. Tommy once told me it's waist-deep for seven miles out in the ocean from land in Key West. Once we saw stingrays and all the jellyfish you would ever want to see as we snorkeled along in the ocean close to the beach. There are many colorful fish and if one goes out far enough, there are many beautiful coral reefs to enjoy. I'm quite the chicken, so our excursions were close to shore in the waist-deep waters. Ha ha.

On one trip, I went shopping as Tommy continued snorkeling. When I returned, he had a great story about how he caught a small shark. I was amazed. It was just another day in the 'Life and Times of Tommy Carter.' We should have written a book.

I loved hearing the stories Tommy and his best friend, Frank, told me about hopping a ride on a tour boat that took them to the deep waters to scuba dive. I was always so impressed they knew how to do all these things. I remember the story Tommy shared over again of how something *really huge* swam by him. We all think it was a whale. How cool is that? Tommy liked to *live* life and not just read about others living life. I admired him for this. For as brave as he was, I was equally a coward. Things were better in the stories I heard and read than in real life for me sometimes.

Oh, I can't forget to pack the cooler with the orange juice, granola bars, and peanut butter and jelly. The staples for our trips. Reservations have been made to stay at the Campgrounds on Marathon Key. I know how to put up the tent and blow up the air mattress Tommy bought for me one year.

I checked my list. I have my E-Z Pass for the toll highways and some cash for when someone doesn't take a credit card. I pack extra drinks and I always bring my Bible and devotionals along. I never leave home without these.

It's time to pack the beach bag. Swimsuit, water shoes, and sunscreen are next. I never thought water shoes were necessary, but they do make walking in shallow water easier. They think of everything these days, that's for sure.

On one of our trips to the Keys, I took notes. Tommy looked at me funny when he saw me scribbling. I didn't have the heart to tell him I needed to have the notes for when I made the trip without him. I didn't want him to think I knew he wouldn't be with me someday when I would take the trip alone. In the book, I noted the mile marker I would leave one highway to travel West to the Florida Turnpike and continue South to US 1 south of Miami to enter the north Keys. The whole trip is almost four hundred miles so it takes at least seven long hours. I took notes for every stop we enjoyed in the Keys.

Finally, the truck's all packed and we're ready to go. I won't be alone. Michael wants to see the Keys again, so I told him he could tag along. He put his things in the back of the truck and we headed south. It was early morning, so it was a little cool. As the day goes on, the warmer the weather becomes. We should make it about halfway before the sun is noticeably hot.

'Are you sure you know the way?' Michael asked with a wry smile. He's always trying to yank my chain. He pretends he's never been with me on this trip before.

'I could drive it with my eyes closed!' I

exclaim as I hold the steering wheel and shut my eyes for a moment.

'I believe you! I believe you!' Michael said with laughter in his voice. 'Now, open those eyes and get us there!'

'We're going to have *such* a good time,' I told Michael. 'Remember the many things Tommy taught me and where all the good spots are? He always had our trips mapped out and I was happy to follow. I never had an agenda before, but my agenda will be to share this with you, again, Michael.'

Michael just smiled and gazed out the window at the beautiful coconut palms that only grow in the warmer weather of South Florida. My mom introduced me to them. They are magnificent with their long flowing fronds and their tall trunks some called their stipe.

I looked up to heaven and said, 'I'm going home, Tommy – or should I say to you, *I'm coming home?* Come with us. Be our guide like you always have been. Please do as I continue to drive the miles ahead of us and leave the many miles behind.' I saw Michael turn and look in the back just to make sure Tommy wasn't with us. I shot 'skinny eyes' his way.

We traveled the long highway to the Keys while Warren Zevon sang *Keep Me In Your Heart For a While*. I sang along. Truth is, I'll keep Tommy and everyone else I loved and lost in my heart FOREVER and ever, not just *a while*.

It's Michael that told me I didn't have to ever lose Tommy, or regain my sanity for that matter, but I think I want to. I want to face each day with the joy of a child and the courage of a giant - just like Tommy did!

I'll let you know what happens next!